The co
niece,
through
I had her squirt
on it.

Short Stories for a Rainy Afternoon

Merry Christmas to
Carolyn & Earl
See you on AOL
Best, (Cordy)
Cordelia Loughead
Dec. 2009

Short Stories
for a
Rainy Afternoon

Cordelia E. Lougheed

SANTA FE

Sunstone books may be purchased for educational, business, or sales promotional use. For information please write:
Special Markets Department, Sunstone Press,
P.O. Box 2321, Santa Fe, New Mexico 87504-2321.

Book design • Vicki Ahl
Body typeface • Baskerville Old Face ■ Display typeface • Tempus Sans ITC
Printed on acid free paper

Library of Congress Cataloging-in-Publication Data

Lougheed, Cordelia E.
Short stories for a rainy afternoon / by Cordelia E. Lougheed.
p. cm.
ISBN 978-0-86534-743-4 (softcover : alk. paper)
I. Title.
PS3612.O7855S56 2010
813'.6--dc22

2009045570

WWW.SUNSTONEPRESS.COM
SUNSTONE PRESS / POST OFFICE BOX 2321 / SANTA FE, NM 87504-2321 /USA
(505) 988-4418 / ORDERS ONLY (800) 243-5644 / FAX (505) 988-1025

Contents

Preface

When I lived on the island of St. Croix in the Virgin Islands, my favorite luxury was sitting in the shade under a palm tree with a book. I loved Ernest Haycock's westerns, and mostly his Western short story book. The romance of New Mexico and Arizona captured me early in the Saturday cowboy matinees at the local movie house. Living on an island thirty miles long and fifteen miles wide was rather confining when you were reading the short story, "Last Stage to Lordsburg," later to become the movie *Stagecoach* with John Wayne.

In 1959 I married Robert Lougheed, and we were making my first trip west, since *The National Geographic* was sending him to the Bell Ranch in New Mexico to sketch some of the quarter horses in their remuda for a horse series he was painting. From that point on, our long trips west took place every October and we always spent some time on the Bell so Bob could paint the cowboys, their horses, and ranch life in general. Finally we took time to look at real estate in Santa Fe, where I now live.

So many short stories would run through my mind, and I would say to myself, "write them down." Life was busy for us on painting trips, and we would end up in Canada, or Montana, and then the stories would slip away, only to be replaced with new story ideas. Finally I took a note from my husband's discipline, and started to type some into the computer. While I was writing, I would become a participant in the stories and would be transported to the different parts of the country where we had traveled in our camper van, like "Route 93" in this book. I like the challenge of developing a beginning to a composition with the theme in the middle, and then putting the idea across with an ending in four or five pages. I even love reading stories myself, especially on a rainy afternoon.

—Cordelia E. Lougheed
Santa Fe, 2009

Angel

My neighbor was one cute, fresh blond, but totally likable, and irresponsible. Angel would have me over for coffee and cake and would just enjoy shocking the hell out of my conservative, square ideals. Her tales were better than any soap opera and almost as unbelievable, since she had more nerve than five of me and had no fear of repercussions and certainly no conscious about her acts.

Her husband, Carlos, was a trucker who would be gone a week and, depending on his pickups, maybe two weeks at a time if he had back-to-back loads. He made good money and was a worker. Angel had a nice house, new auto, and always wore lovely clothes. His reward was a wife that flirted with every male in pants.

She brought some of them home and did not worry about what the neighbors thought. I was one of the neighbors, and I believe she was a bit man crazy, but on the other hand a loyal friend and funny beyond words. Still when she invited me for coffee and cake, I went knowing I was going to be entertained with her daring weekly exploits. It was like reading a book, and jumping into the next chapter with anticipation.

She was so honest with me, I could not help but like her pluck. She never failed to entertain me, especially when Carlos came home unexpectedly and her male guest had just left by ten minutes before his arrival. That was too daring for my weak blood. When she would tell me about these close call events, my hands would get sweaty with my nervous anxiety and they would tremble.

"My, God Angel how can you stand this nerve racking existence?"

She would laugh and say, "I guess I am just lucky."

Well, one night her luck ran out. Carlos lost his shipment because he was too late in making arrangements to pick it up in Wisconsin due to bad weather. He decided to come home for the weekend, and had another pickup on Monday from his own location in Omaha.

He was not allowed to park his truck in front of the house because of the neighborhood covenants that kept all delivery and large trucks off the road. So he had to put it in the vacant lot behind our back alley. I was in my son's bedroom putting his clean clothes on the chair when I saw the big truck back into the lot. There was a strange pickup parked in front of the house, and my hands were getting clammy from my usual nervous fright.

Everything appeared to be normal next door, and the truck was still there in front of the house. It remained until Monday morning, which was two nights, but nothing unusual seemed to happen. As soon as the big truck left around eight AM on Monday, the pickup departed a short time later, and I saw a man rush out like he could not wait to leave.

When Angel phoned me for coffee, I flew out the back

door, since by now I could not imagine what took place over the weekend. Well, Carlos walked in the kitchen and yelled, "Hi babe, I'm home." She said, "I'll be down in a minute." She quickly put on a bathrobe, implied she was just getting into the shower and wondered if he was hungry. No, he had eaten at a diner an hour ago.

Her male friend was scared stiff and sneaked into the spare bedroom. When she and her husband went to bed, he waited until he heard snoring and sneaked downstairs to the basement. Carlos had put the doors on the security system, so he could not open them without tripping the alarm. The windows had wires that told him they too were hooked up to the security connection, so he had no way to sneak out without waking everyone on the street.

After Carlos left for his load on Monday morning at eight AM, lover boy grabbed some toast and jam and gulped down water, since he had not had anything to eat or drink all of Sunday. He was quite upset because his wife would phone the police when he failed to come home for two nights. Sure enough, a patrol car happened to notice the license number on the pickup truck parked in front of the house, and the officer phoned the wife that her husband was all right after he rang the doorbell and talked to him. The officer reported to his wife that her husband had spent the night at Mrs. Angel Quintana's home.

Well, you can imagine what kind of hell he caught. Now lover boy's wife came to Angel's house when Carlos was home, and started screaming at Angel to leave her husband alone, and that he had three kids. Lover boy's wife told Carlos that the police found her husband's pickup truck in front of the house.

Carlos had asked Angel whose truck was out front on the night he arrived home, and she replied it was a friend of my son's who was visiting him for the night.

Carlos started questioning me about the truck, and I did not know a thing, as I wiped my moist hands on my slacks. Then he asked my son if his friend left his pickup out in front of his house while he was visiting? My son had to tell him the truth, that no friend was at the house that night. Then my husband wanted to know what was going on with this truck, and why was the neighbor asking us both these questions, and would someone please enlighten him. My palms were shedding sweat, and my eye tic came back like a clock's movement.

When Angel phoned me for coffee, she said, "I had a wild week, and come on over, and I'll tell you all about it, and show you my black eye."

I told her I was sorry I had to take a rain check, and pass on the offer right now. My nerves were not up to all the excitement, and I had to take a pill and rest in bed.

My son came in with a lemonade and started telling me how some of the guys on the football team used to visit Angel after midnight on occasion, and she charged them twenty dollars each for favors. Now my hands were sweating like a shower, and my tic was blinking like the left-turn signal on my Honda. The football team paid twenty dollars?

"Oh Angel, I am going to offer up a novena for you starting on Sunday, and if Carlos, or any of the football team's parents find out what you have been doing, they are going to kill you. Just in case, I'll plan on a Mass for the dead also. Holy mackerel, Angel, who ever gave you that name?"

Benchmark

When I moved my clothes and suitcases into my new apartment, my life was beginning a new chapter. Once I sold my house there was no turning back, so I bit the bullet and accepted my fate. It was a nice retirement home, so life was going to be easy. They had people to clean your rooms, cook your meals, and certainly provide you with entertainment with a list of bridge, shuffleboard, swimming, and many movies in their theater room. If I got bored here, it would be my own fault.

Having been a head chef in a top Italian restaurant in New York, I was about to start eating meatloaf with mashed potatoes, and peas. My stomach was in for a big shock after all the delicious meals I prepared, and ate myself. My secret spaghetti sauce used to pump my ego up with so much praise.

The first night my next-door neighbor, Hank Sloan, invited me to join him at the dinner table. I held my breath when a plate was slipped under my nose with liver and onions, fried potatoes, and string beans. Now I hold no grudge against liver, but when it resembles the soles of my old hiking boots, and just as tough, my resentment is inclined to surface. I filled up on rolls and blueberry pie. One would rather hope that they would have displayed a nice buffet with a selection, but Hank informed me that this setting was designed to save the home food and money, and us extra monthly expenses.

In the morning we would walk down the path in the garden. There were two rows of benches under the shade trees. The men sat on one side, talking about the baseball game on TV, and the women sat on the other row opposite them, and I could hear a little bit about their hair dye and manicures. Frankly, the baseball and heavyweight fights held no interest for my ears, and one woman's conversation on her hysterectomy and bad permanent left me weak.

My ears did perk up when the new widow asked if anyone had a good recipe for chicken cacciatore. Well, all of the other gals put her down right away, since none of them wanted to even think about cooking. Their days of dishing out food were over. The kids were grown, and most were widows, so now free from the stove, and pots and pans.

I got right up, jumped ship, and slid in next to her on the women's bench. I introduced myself, and informed her that my recipe had been tested on hundreds from *The Queen Mary*, to Salvator's Italian Restaurant in New York. My pad and pencil came right out, and I took her by the arm to the lone bench by the fishpond, and started telling her the ingredients. Well, we exchanged some recipes, and food talk for over an hour, and she could not get enough of my Italian mixtures, She informed me of her love of cooking, which seemed to be a dirty word with the rest of the female population.

We met the next day and went out to lunch so we could discuss our cooking lust for a good meal. I told her how I missed conversing with all the customers who appreciated my special plates, and felt a bit like a celebrity when I would hear their praise of my good sauces.

Since I had all the dishes with the proper ingredients in my head, she suggested I write them all down for her in my spare time. My God, they came flowing out of me like a fountain, and she got every detail, since I even remembered the cooking instructions and the extra care in baking at the correct oven temperatures.

Hank gave me a bit of a hard time because I watched cooking shows instead of the sports on TV, but he had no passion for a perfect mushroom or onion, when I tried to engage him in cooking chatter. He cut me off with, "I'm not interested in that crap." Well, so much for polite conversation, but I did repeat his remark when he informed me that two home runs by the Cleveland Indians won the game in the ninth inning.

Many months passed, and I had settled into the daily routine and enjoyed my morning walk before breakfast.

On the other hand, Barbara could not get enough of the food channels either, so the both of us watched them together at times. She said the chef's daughter was getting married next Saturday, and he was going to freeze some meals for the home, so he could attend. She had mentioned me to him, and asked if I was willing, could I whip them up a nice Italian dinner. He loved the idea, so I told him I would consider it a pleasure to feed the hungry horde Saturday night.

Talk about show biz, for I poured it on with my famous spaghetti sauce, meatballs, and sausage, plus my super garlic bread. When everyone dipped into their plate, I heard words of praise from one end of the dining room to the other, and when I stepped out from behind the kitchen door, I flushed as clapping and cheering greeted me.

Barbara said she had a surprise for me and presented me with a stack of cookbooks with my name splashed across the front as the author. She had taken my photo in the garden one afternoon, and there it was on the cover. Her brother was a publisher and thought it would be a popular book, especially at Christmas, and would sell well to the cooking fans.

Everyone asked Barbara for a copy, and I was handed a pen with a request to sign the books for family members. A book came under my glasses, and when I looked up it was Hank. He mentioned how his daughter liked to cook, and would I please sign her a copy, and by the way, "You sure hit a home run today with the bases loaded."

Barbara gave me a thumbs up, and a big smile. She repeated the lines from Casablanca to me. "I think this is going to be the beginning of a beautiful friendship."

With that, I kissed her hard on the lips with relish—yes, relish.

Cycle of Life

My brother Fred had just moved in with me. His wife had divorced him five years earlier and married an Air Force officer at the nearby base. He thought it would be cheaper for the both of us, but really some company would be a pleasure after living alone for so long. We both liked to eat out, and catch the new movies like we did as kids, though in those days it was just a burger and fries at one of the local burger joints where all the kids hung out. God knows, Fred and I both sat by ourselves in two different homes for years.

My husband had died from a heart attack when he was only forty-two years old, so I had spent a long time alone in this small house. I only had one son, but he joined the army as soon as he graduated from high school and went off to war with his buddies, never to return. My husband's family had money, and in time it filtered down to me, so I had enough for my simple needs.

Fred occasionally went out to dinner with two of his old neighbors, Maude and Jesse Rowe. I was warned that Maude was a witch, and that Fred put up with her just to enjoy Jesse's company, for he was one of Fred's best friends. I soon learned what he meant, because I had to bite my tongue in her presence, since she was what is known as the impossible woman. I think if Fred took the W out of witch and replaced it with a B, he would have the true nature of this gal.

Every time Jess had an opinion, Maude would torpedo his comments with a put down about his knowledge on the subject. He would just smile and continue with his talk. His conversation was directed at Fred, but he would turn to me out of politeness at times. Maude did not confine her nasty nature to her husband alone, because the waiter had to hear her many complaints about the cold coffee, lumps in the mashed potatoes, and the toughness of her steak. My dinner was the same order, since we were in a steak house. Frankly, my coffee, potatoes, and steak stood before me as an A plus meal. Fred informed me that this was her usual restaurant decorum.

When Fred had asked Jesse about Maude's bad behavior one day, Jesse replied that he was stuck with her and had learned to ignore her nasty nature, or he would have to listen to her rant and rave for hours in bed. They were both Catholics, and he had learned to bite the bullet, and hang in there for his reward and salvation in heaven. I wondered if hell on earth was worth the gamble.

The next meal out took place in a fine Italian restaurant, and I went along for Fred's sake, and truly found Jesse very smart, interesting, and I could see why Fred loved his company. His knowledge of solar energy was amazing, and he did not waste his engineering degree on building a better mousetrap. He was into Sci Fi things that would be future necessities as the population grew. He mentioned all the shortages of plain water that had already begun to affect parts of the world, and gave us the details of a new machine that would extract fresh water moisture out of the air and drain it into a storage tank. It would contain no bad chemicals, since it would not run through contaminated ground. He reminded us of the new present oxygen machines that now eliminated the old heavy tanks that had to be exchanged when they were empty, and what a job it was to lug them into a sick room. The oxygen was in the air we breathed, so the machine could take it from nature, and produce it twenty-four hours a day in your own bedroom and could keep a respiratory patient alive without the help of the old fashion heavy metal cylinder exchange.

We loved listening to him tell us the new wonders on the horizon, but Maude was not going to sit back and let her husband hold court on these revelations to Fred and me. She had to interrupt with complaints on the spaghetti size, and she wanted the thinner pasta. Also, her spaghetti sauce was bitter, and the waiter apparently slipped her regular coffee instead of decaf, so it would keep her awake all night. I later mentioned to Fred that I was starting to think she was jealous of her husband's charm, sense of humor, and intelligence. He had thought the same thing until he was in their home one night to drop off a book, and Maude was as mean as a skunk with her nice daughter and son. The water pump in the car went out in her car when the boy was driving it to the store, which could have happened to any older auto. She treated him like he personally did it on purpose and made him work after school to pay for it, and would not speak to him for two weeks. That sounded like mental illness to me, but Fred said her doctor said she was just mean and controlling, and it seemed to be her normal behavior.

Well, everything came to light one night at dinner. Never did Maude take a drink with our dinners out, but this evening she kept ordering drinks and she started downing one after another. When she ordered another vodka on the rocks, Jesse told the waiter, "No." The poor fellow did not know what to do, and walked away from the table. This put Maude in a rage, and she started yelling at Jesse at the top of her lungs, and began screaming obscenities at her husband and the waiter. Everyone in the place turned their heads and held their conversations, as this mad woman went crazy, until Jesse had to lift her out of the chair and drag her out to the car. She went wild, and was hitting him, and scratching his face with her nails, until blood ran down on his white shirt. Fred had to drive so Jesse could hold her down in the back seat.

I followed in our car so I could pick up Fred, and Jesse pulled her out of the car with her screams drifting through the neighborhood, until people came out on their porches to see who was getting killed. Both of the kids' faces were at the upstairs windows, and you could tell that they were mortified with shame.

A few days later Fred met Jesse in town for lunch, and he confessed his life was a nightmare, since Maude had been in and out of alcohol rehab hospitals on and off for most of their marriage. She would stop for a month at most, and the hell would begin again. He had spent a fortune on her treatment to no avail, and finally told her this was her last chance, because if she did not keep dry this time, he was taking the kids and moving out. No judge would let the children be exposed to her abuse in the future.

We met Jesse and the kids for Sunday brunch on a rainy afternoon, and what a peaceful meal it was without the complaining and interruptions that Maude usually managed to inflict on everyone. The daughter Sheila told me how she wanted to study art, and son Hank wanted to take engineering like his dad. While the men were talking, Sheila told me she could invite her girlfriend to her home and not worry about her mother humiliating her now that she was in rehab.

Jesse thought the battle was won after two months of a dry run for Maude, but a trip home one evening found her passed out on the bed with a vodka bottle on the nightstand. There was no glass, and lipstick surrounded the top of the bottle as she just took it in straight gulps. She was conked out dead cold drunk until morning. Then she was informed that they were moving out of the house, and she could drink herself sick and she would be on her own.

They rented a condo and invited us for Thanksgiving dinner. Sheila was doing all the cooking herself and would not let me bring a thing, so I bought her a fine art book. She was 16 now, and I told her how great she was to take on such an undertaking. She laughed and said, "Who do you think has been cooking our Christmas and Thanksgiving dinners these past number of years? I learned from the TV cooking shows, and my father helped me, and we both did the dinners on most nights." She thought that anything that is learned even under hard circumstances is never wasted, and I informed her, "You will make a fine wife and mother."

Maude had alcohol-induced dementia and could not take care of herself, so Jesse had to put her in a nursing home as more expenses fell upon his back. They moved back into their own home, and life moved on.

Jesse, Fred and I still had our dinners out, usually on Saturday night, but on the side, Jesse and I were dating, and we really enjoyed one another's company. The future seemed dim for the both of us, but at our age we settled for companionship and what love we could share. Our friendship seemed to fill a need in our lives, and we reconciled ourselves to the realization that this would be the best out of life that we could manage under the circumstances.

When Jesse got sick with liver cancer, I filled in for the nurse to give her a break at times, and I read to him, fed him and gave him love. Both the kids were now in college and could not get home often to see him, but they phoned and wrote every chance they could. He passed away on a cold February day, and by Fred's face, and tone I knew what words came over the phone line.

We were both moping around the house that week, when Fred told me to get my coat. He drove us to the new Roadhouse Restaurant, so we were back to our usual dinner out. He informed me that a new movie was waiting for us at the local mall, and we headed for the parking lot.

The third cycle of life for Fred and me was just starting, and I was grateful my mother decided to try for another child and produced a brother named Fred.

Dude Ranch

Vacation was coming up, and I had been saving money for a year. Last summer I missed out on a chance to head west with my friend, Rita. She raved about the dude ranch in Montana, so that whet my appetite to go with her this year. We both received two weeks in July for our vacation. I just could not afford it, until I wised up and stopped smoking and drinking in the bars with the gang, cut down on eating out and going to the movies. I could not believe how much money of my salary went down the drain until I saw the huge amount of bills in the kitty jug. Not only could I afford the trip, but a new wardrobe with good-looking jeans, western boots, and a swell Stetson hat.

Rita and I checked into our nice cabin and went to dinner at the main building, which contained the front desk, a small store with a few handy items like sunscreen, aspirin, candy and some straw hats. The dining room was located on the far end of the hall near the office, and that was where we were headed.

We were introduced to everyone at the long table by the ranch manager in charge. There were twelve in our group, including a young city slicker, a pilot, lawyer, post office worker, and dentist in the male group, and the rest were females with their husbands and children. There were two young single girls on the make, who were eyeing the two cowboys that would take us on the ride tomorrow morning. These gals never paid anyone else attention and were putting all their best effort into flirting and gushing over the two hands. The other men were in their late thirties or early forties, so the girls had no interest in them.

We got through a good breakfast and all met at the stable to get our instructions on handling the horses. They were already saddled, and the young cowboys helped us new riders mount properly from the left side and showed us how to turn the stirrup on the side, so our foot would slip into it easily. Some horses could move a few paces forward, and this way, you would be facing the rear and step up quickly and throw your right leg over the saddle. This done, they showed us how to use the reins to turn the horse, and told us not to hold them too tight unless you wanted to stop. Rita knew all this, but let the cowboy show it to her again, and that way she could look him over and talk to him.

Off we went, and the horses were very gentle with us amateurs. As we climbed the green hills, the high altitude sun was quite penetrating so I was glad for my hat and sunscreen on my arms. I could see some bad burns on arms of a few riders, and one fellow with a baseball cap had a flaming red neck that would need some attention tonight.

After we had a sandwich and drink, we mounted again and headed for a path in the trees for some shade. The blond gal pushed her horse by me and yelled, "Move aside, stupid." Well that got the hackles up on my neck, but I decided to not let her ruin my vacation. She also gave me some dirty looks earlier when Kyle was riding alongside me while we visited. She pushed by Rita on the narrow trail in the woods to catch up to Kyle's horse.

At dinner, a few daggers darted our way because Hank and Kyle sat between Rita and me. Hank wondered where we were from, and what jobs we held in Greenwich, Connecticut. The blond came up behind Kyle and invited him and Hank to their cabin for drinks after dinner. He had to inform her that it was against regulations to visit single women in their residence. She turned and walked off in a huff. She and the girlfriend sat at the opposite end of the table giving us their double barrel evil eye for a half hour. Rita whispered in my ear that they were spoiled New York bitches.

The morning air was lovely as we rode through the aspen trees, and were heading for a good shady spot where we could sit on some large rocks and eat the boxed lunches the ranch prepared. We all carried our own box behind our saddle, and it was very tasty. We got to visit with some of the other people with their kids, and they were having a wonderful time.

When we were ready to mount up again, I remembered the proper procedure, and threw my leg over the saddle like a horsewoman, and was shocked when the horse reared up throwing me over his rump to the ground. Every man came to my aid, and I was on my feet in minutes and more surprised than hurt.

Rita had just put her weight down a minute after me, and her horse nickered and took off down the path through the trees. She tried to slow him down and was yelling at him as she was pulling on the reins. He was unstoppable and continued at breakneck speed through the trees. When he veered around a rock, a low hanging branch struck her in the forehead and knocked her right out of the stirrups. Kyle was already mounted and on her trail, followed by Hank.

When they got to her, she was unconscious in a heap. The boys had to get Rita in Kyle's saddle with him behind her limp form and have him put his arms around her waist to hold her steady as he walked the horse back to the office so they could get her to the hospital ten miles away.

Hank came back with her horse, and said, "Something is not right when you have two horses spooked like that." When he took off the saddles, he found a large carpet tack under the saddle blanket on each horse with blood around them.

It was obvious some person put them there, and my mind went right to the bitchy blond and her girl friend.

Hank said, "Play it cool and don't say anything. You need proof, or they can sue you."

When we got to town and the hospital, the doctor said Rita was still unconscious because her skull had a bad fracture, and the x-ray showed blood behind it. To ease the pressure on the brain, they had to operate and drain it. She had a good chance of being normal with the above procedure.

Hank and Kyle agreed with me about the blond and girlfriend because they noticed the way they pushed their horses ahead of us on the trail. Also, the dirty looks were very noticeable. We decided to sneak up to the girl's cabin and get next to the open window in the sitting room. Kyle knocked on their door and kept them on the porch while they asked him about the poor girl that was injured, and how was she doing at the hospital? He gave them a report and mentioned that Hank had found tacks under the saddles. There was a pause and they both said, "Really?" He then left the both of them standing there acting uncomfortable and guilty and headed to the main building.

Then they both started talking and yelling at one another in the small room. The friend blared, "Damn you, Sue I told you not to put those tacks under the saddles, and I'm not taking a rap for murder if that girl dies."

The blond turned on her, and yelled, "If they find out, it will be because of your big mouth. No one saw me, so they can't prove I did it. Just keep that damn mouth of yours shut."

Hank had his recorder taping and grabbed my arm to leave. We tiptoed quietly down to the main building. The four of us sat in the small office while Hank turned on the recording for Kyle. We all looked at one another with the expression, "What are we going to do about it?" We piled into Hank's truck, drove to the police station, and played the tape for the Captain. When the officer brought both girls into the station, he played the tape separately to them. First was the girlfriend of the blond, and she started crying in fear and immediately condemned her blond friend as doing it while we all had lunch. She kept saying, "I told her not to do that because it was very dangerous to the riders and could also hurt the horses."

When the blond heard what her friend said, she blamed it on her because she was very jealous of Rita. Then they played the tape to her and announced, "You are under arrest. You have the right to remain silent," and so forth.

We drove to the hospital in the morning, and the ranch called off their morning ride because of the accident and probably the rain. Rita had regained consciousness and looked terrible with her head shaved and completely wrapped in a white ball of gauze. They only let us stay a few minutes and did not want her to talk. The doctor thought she would be all right with the pressure off the brain.

Kyle went back the next day and could stay for twenty minutes. He explained how the blond was under arrest and her rich parents were flying out to get a lawyer. He held her hand for the whole time he sat next to her. She was thrilled.

Hank's father's friend was a good lawyer, and he and the blond's attorney would converse and decide what was best for both clients. As it turns out, the lawsuit might take place, so the parents and the lawyer would offer Rita a good sum of money for a settlement if she did not press charges and sue. Rita was to get a million dollars and have them pick up the medical bills beyond her own coverage.

Rita could now sit up and talk, and Kyle kept her company when he could get away from his job. I had to fly back home to go back to work, and Hank asked me to write to him. When I went to the hospital to say goodbye to Rita, I said, "I'll see you back in Greenwich."

She said, "No you won't. When I was in Greenwich I lived in that lousy attic apartment with Claire, and it was on the third floor and very dark and dreary. I did without many things so I could afford to come out west where I always wanted to live. Now I have money in the bank here, thanks to Kyle getting me all the bank forms. I'm getting better and have a cowboy at my side, and frankly I am quite happy. Come visit me when I get settled, and tell Claire to send my clothes, and I'll send her a check. She can keep my earthly goods, like the television and stereo. This trip has taught me the value of good friends, and the God Almighty power of a million dollar carpet tack."

Father's Day

The nice looking man in the office would smile at me every time our eyes met, which seemed to be quite frequently lately. This went on for a few weeks, and then one day he asked if I would like to have lunch with him at the spaghetti place on the corner. Of course I would, for he was a nice, clean cut looking gentleman, and a snappy dresser.

We were both a bit shy, but finally loosened up enough to talk our heads off, and had so much to say that we had to make another date so we could get it all out. This went on for six months, and I never knew two people could exchange so much information about their lives and childhood. By then we were thick as thieves and went to the movies, and out to dinner with a few picnics thrown in on romantic weekends.

He presented me with a lovely diamond, and the engagement did not last long, since we could hardly wait to get married. We did not tell anyone of our plans, but we flew to Nevada for a long weekend and found it easy to obtain a legal marriage certificate. Coming back on the plane, we both had shiny new wedding bands on our fingers, and I moved right into his apartment.

It did happen very fast, and with all our conversation,

and smarts, for some reason we never did discuss having children. Our talks were on travel and food we liked, to our favorite books and movies, and some politics. However, we did not talk of the future, which was beyond being dumb. Well, when I announced I was pregnant, it was like presenting him with a two-ton elephant in our lives. He said he did not plan on having a family, and of course, I asked why he never mentioned it to me.

My nice slim looks changed as the months rolled away, and his affection went with it out the window. I had to stay home, and when the doctor took the ultrasound, he smiled and announced I was going to have twin boys. When I passed this news on to my husband, he walked out of the house and went to the corner bar to tell the bartender his troubles, I presumed.

My one good friend in the office, Marie Montoya, was very happy for me, and we would talk on the phone for a long time about motherhood, and life in general, and she gave me warm comfort. By then Jim came home late at night, with one excuse or another, from working late to playing bridge with his old club members. It took a while for Marie to tell me about the new good-looking gal that worked in accounting. It seems that they would have lunch together, and since she did not know Marie and I were friends, started telling her about her love life with my husband. It gave me the most helpless feeling in the world, and I tried to hang on to my disorderly life so the worry would not drag my spirits down as I moved into my last months before giving birth.

As soon as I became a mother, I rented an apartment of my own and just moved out one day when Jim was off with the new girl friend over the weekend. Bless my father, for he had left me some money and securities when he recently died, so I was still mourning him and my miserable marriage.

Jim came home to the empty apartment, and realized I was gone, but he must have figured we were finished for good, since I did not even leave him a note. My only message was the bare closets, and the missing suitcase.

I was so busy with the two babies, I did not even miss him. Once I had heard about the girlfriend in the office, my mind shut down on him as a big mistake in my life, but had to thank him for producing my two lovely boys.

Finally, my lawyer sent him the divorce papers, and he gave up all legal claim to his sons, and I moved on with my life. The babe in the office dropped him because he was not interested in another marriage, and he told her he had no interest in having a family. She met some other fellow at her gym club, and they moved to Ohio with their new baby.

My boys were now old enough to talk and be little fun boys, and how I worshipped them in my life. As they grew a little older, I found I was a soccer mom and went to all their games. I now worked from the house and could arrange my time so I would not miss any of their events. They also played basketball on occasion, and baseball in season, so a lot of my time was spent cheering them on in one sport or another.

At the doctor's office, my tests results came back, and I had a serious problem that needed treatment. The boys were quite worried, and I did not know who would take care of them while I had an operation.

Marie mentioned this to Jim one day in the office, and he was quite surprised to hear she was friendly with me. When the doorbell rang, one of the boys answered it and let their father in the living room. I was totally surprised, for I had never heard one word from him in these many years. When I introduced the boys to their father as their father, they looked at one another like a strange bomb had just exploded in their lives.

The meeting was quite awkward for all of us, until the boys started telling him about their sports and how much they loved playing soccer, baseball, and so forth, and their favorite team was the Yankees. Jim was floored, for he still thought I had a couple of babies and had no idea he actually had young boys that like sports, for he too was a Yankee fan. They spent the whole night talking baseball, and I excused myself to go in the bedroom, since my clock said eight-thirty, and the man I was going to marry was phoning me from London in five minutes. He had a job for his company there for six months and was trying to wind it up early. I told him not to worry because this operation was a simple routine one, and I would probably be home in a week and in better health when he returned to the States.

My boys were crazy about Don, and he was like a father to them, since he also went to their games, and took them to the Boston Red Sox games when they played the New York Yankees, and he even took them to the Series when he managed to get tickets. They truly loved him and asked about him all the time.

When Jim asked me when I was going to the hospital and who was taking care of the boys, I had to say I still did not have that pinned down. I could have fallen over when he said he could take care of them because he had a week off from work coming to him. The boys thought that was all right, but he was still a stranger to them, so they were going to be polite and put their time in with him until I came home.

After no years of contact with them, they were suspicious of him, for why would he not bother with them before this time? They had always asked about their father, and I did not say anything bad about him. They just know he lived in the same city, but had some problems in his life and could not be a father to them. Of course they did not understand, and were not that interested now that they had Don as their father.

My operation came off fine, and the prognosis was good for the future, so I just held my breath until Don's return. He loved me and the boys and had bought a house in Orlando, so we could all live in that city once we were married and he was transferred to his new position there.

In the mean time, Jim kept coming over to see his sons and started going to their games, so he could watch them play. At times, he mentioned that maybe we should get back together, but I skirted that conversation. I stayed in the background, went to their games by myself, and faded into the stands so he could not see me. I did not want to complicate my life now that my future looked so bright.

Time moved along, and we were waiting for Don's plane to land, and the boys and I were truly excited about the prospects of our new life in the south. When he came into the building, I ran to him, and we had our long awaited kiss and hug, with the boys putting their arms around the both of us. That certainly made us feel like a family. Don wanted to get married right away and said we were getting our license tomorrow.

We four went to the Judge's chambers, who would perform the ceremony. He was a college friend of Don's. When I heard the words, "I now pronounced you man a wife," we all gave kisses to one another in our happiness.

We had to go back to our apartment to just get the last few suitcases to take them to the airport. The movers had already taken our things by truck that morning. As we were going out the door, Jim walked up to the boys and asked his sons if they were playing soccer in the late afternoon, for the team was scheduled to play at four, and he did not want to miss seeing his boys on the field. They told him they were sorry, but they were going to their new home, since their mother was just married that morning. The boys started telling him that they were now moving to a new house in Florida, and they were leaving the team. You could see the new world that just opened to Jim collapse in his expression.

The boys introduced Don to him. "This is our father, Don Crosby, and he is a great soccer player and coach."

Jim shook his hand, and I saw a tear roll down the corner of his eye, as we walked down the long hallway and out of his life forever.

Midlife

In thirty years of marriage, never did Jeff and I ever take a trip alone. Always friends and neighbors, Burt and Selma, joined us for the foursome, and our kids stayed with relatives or baby sitters. We went to the national parks and camped together, flew to Vegas, the Canyon, Hawaii, and every other place we wanted to visit. We did have a lot of fun and would sit in bars drinking and laughing, and busting at the seams.

Lately, Jeff seemed a bit distracted and did not feel like doing much together around the yard, or in the house. I just thought he was getting older and maybe having a bit of male menopause. It seemed to go on for quite a while, and his spirit was restless as the months moved by.

Then a trip to The Florida Keys came up, and the boys did some vacation shifting with other workers, and we four were off for some sun and fun. As we drove here and there looking at the quaint back roads on the island, I suddenly got my mind into focus when we would eat and settle down for a drink in the late afternoon. I noticed that Jeff would laugh the loudest at Selma's jokes. Also, he would move faster than Burt to hold the car door for her, and there appeared to be much smiling back and forth between them. I had to ask myself if I was putting things together or had they always been that way. I'm sure I would have noticed it through the years.

When we got home, Jeff had to run to the Depot for a new tool he needed in the garage, or something for the yard. He would disappear for an hour or so, and come back with a small shopping bag. Then my female brain said, phone Selma and see if she is home right now. Burt would answer and tell me she went to the grocery store.

I finally got my little VW fixed, so we again had two cars. I waited until our Ford pulled out and rounded the corner, and I hung back and followed it. Sure enough, he met Selma in the parking lot at some little bar where the four of us never visited, and when I peeked in the window, I could see them in a booth holding hands. Well, you can imagine my shock.

This went on for a little while, and one night when they were together, I dragged Burt with me to see what was going on. He was overwhelmed with rage and totally mortified. It took the both of us by surprise because we had known one another for thirty years and never had any idea our spouses were attracted to each other.

Well, it ran its course, and pretty soon I had to face Jeff with the known facts, and he buckled under then and finally asked me for a divorce. Who wants to be married to someone that does not want to be with you, not me. So I played hardball financially, getting the house, but gave in on some of our stocks and savings, since his lawyer and mine worked out the agreement. Poor Burt had to take out a mortgage on their house, just after he had finished paying the thirty-year loan on the place. She received the money for her half of the house, the car, and part of some money they had invested, but less than she wanted, for his lawyer said, you get the half value of the house and can't take it all.

Jeff and Selma set up housekeeping in an apartment on the other side of town, so we really did not run into them. Burt came over for dinner once in a while, and we would both cry in a beer or two, and shake our heads in disbelief. Then some nights we would talk, and I realized in all the years of travel together, and being in his company, I never really knew the man. He told me how Selma could never sit home and would drag him to every new movie or event that took place that had an interest for her. He said he would love to stay home, just read some new books and watch an old movie on TV. I had to say that Jeff was very much like Selma, and I only got to a book after the kids went to school, and loved that quiet time.

He would come over with a novel that we both wanted to read together, so we could discuss it, and would take turns reading out loud eight pages each. My God, that was fun, and we got into what we thought was the meaning and analyze the ending, thinking it should have been this way or that way. We liked the same type of movies, and especially the old ones in black and white where the stories were about people with human interest. No science fiction with crazy car bombs, and men that were part machine that could throw cars across the street, like Selma wanted to see. As a matter of fact, Jeff liked that junk too. I can't tell you how many lousy movies with chain saw murders or flying vampires I sat through in thirty years. Sitting at home with the fireplace going and reading our books was like an evening of magic culture that my system seemed to require. You never know how much you can enjoy something unless you are exposed to it. Now for the first time in my life, I really think I found the contentment I always missed, and it fell into my lap due to a jerk husband and my old friend being selfish, and putting their needs ahead of their marriage vows. Thank God, Selma wanted Jeff and not some good-looking waiter at the hotel, or I would have missed this new adventure in reading and companionship with Burt.

As we both drew closer, we started looking forward to our relationship, and it moved into act three when he kissed me goodnight after a dinner and reading. Then it moved into a peaceful love at our age, and we hung on to it and started planning for our future. Our kids had left the nest a few years back and had lives of their own, with their children and jobs.

We decided to get married, but out of town, so it would be just our business, and we would work out the living arrangements later. If Burt could sell his house, it would be a blessing because he could pay off the new mortgage, and we could decide where we both wanted to live. In fact we even discussed moving out of state, since Burt could work any place with the same insurance company. Thus, over a long weekend we were able to drive to a southern state and be joined as husband and wife.

Even though we were married, we still lived in our own homes until we could get his off the market. When he came for dinner and told me Selma met him at the office door as he was walking to the car, I was quite surprised. He thought she needed more money, or some information, but was knocked off balance when she mentioned her arrangement with Jeff was not working out. It seemed she was happier with him in their house. She offered to pay off the new mortgage if he would take her back. Burt told her to meet him at our old bar tomorrow evening at six and bring Jeff. I thought he wanted to think it over and drop me, but that was not it. He now loved me, and we were married, and he had a big surprise to tell me tomorrow night at Mac's Bar and Grill. That worried me plenty, because all he had to tell her was that we were now married, but he wanted both Selma and Jeff there together to announce it, I supposed.

Burt had been absolutely gushing with some news, but was saving it, so I thought he managed a transfer to Arizona. That is where he wanted to live, and it sounded good to me too. In fact one of my kids in the next town was renting a condo, and it was much too expensive. He wanted to make a deal with me and buy my house, so if we were going to Arizona, he would have his old homestead again.

We walked into the bar all smiles, and I don't think they even knew I was friendly with Burt anymore. The both of them did not look happy, and Jeff did not look me in the eyes. Selma took right over and told Burt that she and Jeff ran their course, and she realized it was a big mistake and was ready to pay off the mortgage for her half of the house and start all over. Jeff finally looked at me and said he was very sad for running out on me, but it was just a crazy time in life at his age, and he was looking for something new. He did not deserve a second chance, but maybe I could see it in my heart to take him back.

Burt looked Selma in the face up close and said he really hated being dragged out of his comfortable home night after night for Bingo, terrible movies, and church dances he deplored. At last he had found comfort and never knew how wonderful and restful life could be until now.

Then he smiled and said, "It's just too bad about you

two damn fools, but you did both of us a big favor, and my new wife and I have plans for a whole new environment in Arizona." With that, he bent me over in a kiss that broke the record for any I ever received, even in high school. Two amazed people stared at each other, and Burt waved some hundred dollar bills in their noses, and announced. "I've already paid the mortgage off and will take my Lotto money to some property outside of Tucson and build our new house on the desert with a big library and home movie theater. I'm afraid you two are stuck with one another, and it looks like that is not going to be a happy union in your old age. My foursome days are over. Now, it's just Rita and me."

We both danced out of there arm in arm and never turned back to see the sad faces that hung over their stale beer. My God, we felt good.

Molly and Me

Molly and I were sitting in the drug store eating a club sandwich and drinking a coke, talking about meeting some nice prospects for husbands soon, since we wanted to get married and have children while we were still young. Two sailors sat at the nearby counter and ordered two chocolate sodas. We looked them over carefully, and both were quite clean cut looking. One was cute and the other rather handsome. It took them a while to notice us, but they got around to it and flashed a smile at our table.

By the time they got into their drinks, they started asking us questions about the town since they both just arrived at their new station. In an hour we had them at our table, with a date for the local movie at four o'clock. It seems that they were not sailors, but two members of the U.S. Coast Guard, and proud of it.

They were going to be working at the lighthouse, so Greg could man the light, radio, and fog horn, and they would be living on the island of rock with the very large house located a mile out from shore. Molly was very interested in hearing about the big house out in the sound. Greg, the cute one, could hardly wait to fill her in because he thought it was a very nice building, The kitchen had been done over and was quite modern. They had satellite TV with a large screen, plus very comfortable living quarters. The other Coast Guard residents were leaving for a new post, so they had been showing Greg the ropes and what had to be done to work the light and clean the gears that ran the motor that revolved the beacon, and also learn how to use the new radio and polish the equipment. They were due to take it over by themselves in another week.

They were going to have us out for dinner once they were in charge and would pick us up in the supply boat at the dock on next Saturday.

Well, Molly thought Greg was perfect and announced to me that I should not be surprised if she married him in the future. I told her she was crazy because she would be living on that dumb island and not getting into town to shop, or eat in the restaurants, or go to the movies when she wanted, because they would only be coming in for food and mail maybe once or twice a week. She said how much she would love to live out there and cook in that big kitchen with the Coast Guard buying the food and paying the rent.

Frankly, I thought Roy was a good catch, for he was easy going, funny, and good looking. He would meet me in town as time went on and come to my apartment for a bite to eat, and we would talk about everything. Sometimes we would go to the movies and grab a bite out, and he told me he was most happy when we were together. Well, some of his goodnight kisses were hot stuff, and it did not take him too long to mention, "Maybe we should think of a permanent union in the future."

Well, after that first trip to the lighthouse, I decided I

was not going to get buried out there on that slab of rocks and sit in the fog for days while that bloody foghorn blew over my head. I did not tell him that, though, because I liked our arrangement. When he did bring me a small diamond and asked for my hand in marriage, I let him know I loved him, but could not stand to live in the confinement of that lighthouse. After all, I would be stuck there until the boat had to come to the dock for supplies, and I was used to going to the movies, library, and visiting my friends on dry land. I tried to talk him into marriage and spending a night here in my apartment, so we could be near the activity of the town. He told me he wanted a wife with him for breakfast and dinner.

He was too good to lose, so I told him we would talk about it in the future, and maybe work out a deal where I could spend a few nights out there, and the other time in my apartment. We kept dating, but he was not happy that I did not want to be with him where he was based. In the meantime, we stood up for Molly and Greg, and they spent their honeymoon in town at the motel and then moved Molly out to the island. This put pressure on me, for the house was big enough for two couples out there, and had four bedrooms. Molly got pregnant right away, so they fixed up the extra small bedroom for the baby.

Roy would come see me when he came to town to get food for the week's supply, but we both missed one another during the week. After a while, he came to town but did not always visit me, and I was afraid I would lose him. I would worry about it, and then he would show up for a dinner and visit. Our romance was going no place.

The winter and spring flew by, and in the Fall Molly had

a cute baby girl. She came into town to have lunch with me, and I asked her how she liked living on the rock. She just loved it, and Greg was great with the baby and could take care of her so she could come to town for our lunch once in a while. I asked about Roy, because he had not phoned me in a long time, and she mentioned that he went home on leave to see his family and would not be back for another week. When the week was up, I wanted to get back together with him and talk more of our marriage. I realized he was going to slip through my fingers if I played too hard to get.

Molly was sick and missed coming into town for three weeks, so she could not have lunch with me. Finally, when she stopped coughing, she felt she could meet me for a meal at my apartment.

I wanted to know if she saw Roy and was he back as yet, but the answer was, no. He did not come back to the lighthouse because he was trained in high tech work, and they needed him in Hawaii on a special job.

I said, "Hawaii, is he going to stay there long?" She thought so, because the Coast Guard gave him a swell house near the base, and he told Greg he expected to be there for four years on the project.

I asked if Greg could give me his address, and Molly said, "I have it here."

I was going to write him right away and tell him I could fly to Hawaii in a week and marry him in Honolulu where he was stationed. I waited for his reply, and even packed my favorite clothes in boxes so I could send them to his address. A week went by, and I would run home from my job at noon to check the mail. Two more weeks went by, and there was still no letter to me, and I figured my letter went by boat, and not by air, so I guessed it would arrive as soon as they sorted it out in Honolulu.

After a month, there was a five-by-seven envelope in my box, and I had goose bumps as I ran the opener along the back seam at the top. I figured he sent me my airplane ticket and could hardly wait to rip into the letter. When I pulled the stationery from the brown manila, out came a photo with it, and it said Roy and Betty Bower, with the date of their marriage.

Molly had to tell me it was his school sweetheart, and they got back together when he went home on leave. She also told me, "You were a fool to string Roy along, and not move out to the lighthouse, because he was only there to show Greg the ropes on the complicated radio. They had a replacement coming with his wife and child as soon as he was finished. He did not tell you that, because he wanted to see if you loved him enough to move out on the island with him. You failed the test by being selfish about leaving town. You are a damn fool, Liz, and I won't be able to have lunch with you in town after the summer, because we will be flying to Hawaii for our next base, and will have a house near Betty and Roy. They hope to start their family there. Roy put Greg's name in for the project, and they relocated us to the island."

I started crying and kicking the packed boxes and calling myself a dumb blond, and Molly agreed with me wholeheartedly.

New Teacher

It was a small cross corners town in Montana, and the KOH brand, King Of Heart's Ranch, was the closest one to town. In fact, our south fence bordered the town line. Mr. Farley named it that when he bought it on a winning poker hand.

The main street contained a short row of old buildings on the dirt wagon tracks that passed east by the log schoolhouse. There was a food store where we picked up our supplies and mail, plus a utility store that had boots, jackets, bullets, knives, grain, and fencing supplies. The saloon was on the corner and popular with the men when they came to town to shop. The food store had a kitchen in the back with tables, and Mrs. Potter baked wonderful pastry to serve with her coffee and tea, and cocoa when the children came with their parents. The Potter kids all handled the cups, sandwiches, and one hot meal a day. If it was a pot roast day, that was served until they ran out of it, but usually, they cooked enough for evening dinner. Leftovers became part of the sandwich menu the following day. The food was good, and it was a real treat to get off the cookhouse diet once in a while.

The schoolhouse had been empty for a year since the

last teacher from the east married a rancher from Wyoming. The log building had a classroom in the front, with a living quarters in the back. It contained a bed, cook stove, and sink with a hand pump to the well. A table and chairs took up the corner near the window, and someone donated a metal tub that would afford a shallow bath on Saturday night.

Now that a new young lady from Boston was about to arrive, the ranch kids could go back to school in September. The surrounding cowboys were anxious to get a look at her, since single women were scarce in the area.

The railroad tracks were slightly north of town with just a sign that said, Powell Montana, named after one of the first ranch owners in this district. The train would stop at the sign on rare occasions to let someone off, or you would flag it down if you wanted to depart, and the train engineer always slowed down to see if anyone was standing next to the sign.

We were all working the fall round up and were camping near the chuck wagon at night. Mr. Farley usually went into town for the mail and some supplies, but had a sore foot from gout this past week and could hardly put any weight on his right food to walk. He asked me to take the wagon, do his run to the store for mail, and pick up a large bag of flour and some sugar for the kitchen. Our location was an easy ride to the stores, so he gave me his wagon with his fast-stepping team of blacks, and they were a pleasure to handle because they were a perfect matched pair and knew the trail by heart.

When I walked in the store and picked up the items, I deposited the food in the wagon, and the mail in the leather pouch. My stomach was looking forward to a coffee and pie before heading back on the trail, so I put my order in with

Mrs. Potter. A lovely girl around nineteen or twenty sat in front of a plate of stew, and Mrs. Potter introduced me to the new schoolteacher. I was so shy and tongue-tied, I only managed to say hello and sat at a table next to her. I immediately ordered stew, so I could sit there longer and linger over my pie and coffee.

I was the only true cowboy she had ever seen, except for a few in magazines. While I was sneaking glances at her, I could see her eyes scan my boots, and Stetson hat on the chair. She started asking me about ranch life, and how she would have to learn how to ride horseback if she wanted to explore the hills above town. Then she asked if I liked to read and told me she had a box full of books coming, and would let me borrow some when she unpacked them. I jumped in and told her I loved to read and would like to see her selection. Also, my pony, Jake, was a gentle horse, and I could give her some riding lessons when I could get off the ranch in the late afternoon if it was OK with her.

She said to come by the schoolhouse and knock on her back door, and she would get ready any afternoon I could spare.

When I had free time, I would meet her late in the day for coffee and one of Mrs. Potter's fruit tarts. The other hands would slip in for coffee at times, but we would ignore them, since I read one of her novels, and she was interested in my opinion of the story. Frankly, reading that book was work, and I had to use every free minute I could spare to get through it, because I was one slow reader. It was homework for my persistent challenge, and I knew I had to get the story down so I could let her know how I enjoyed it. By the time I finished, my mind was full of the story of the family in Australia trying to grow food and survive in a new country. I enjoyed reading about their struggle and how they mastered the harsh climate.

Ruth seemed to like me, and I was love sick over her, and very nervous with all the other hands trying to move into her circle. Ruth never seemed to take much notice of them like I did.

When I walked her to the back door of the schoolhouse, she grabbed my head and pulled it down to her five-by-four frame, and kissed me goodnight. No sleep ever captured my eyes that whole long night, and by morning I worked in a daze most of the day and fell on my bunk early and slid into a lovely sleep with only good dreams of her.

The next time we met, she started asking me where the married cowboys lived on the ranch, and I mentioned they had their own small houses lumped together near the headquarters. She asked if she could visit the ranch in ten days on the weekend. She felt her riding was now good enough to saddle her the ten miles, and she could get there by noon. The fact that she was interested in the married cowboys lifted my heart with the hope that marriage had crossed her mind, so I would pursue the subject when I felt the moment was right.

The weather was nice because it was a lovely fall morning, and I had told her we would meet at the gate by the headquarters, and I would have the cookhouse make us some sandwiches for a little picnic near the pond.

By noon a strong cool wind came up, and I became worried when she did not arrive, especially since it was a lonely trail from town. It became quite cold, so I headed out on Jake and started looking for her on Gentle Jim, for he was so easy in his gait and trot, she would not have any trouble with his ride.

She was nowhere in sight, so I figured the weather scared her off and she turned back as it got cold with the harsh wind. By the time I put Jake in Potter's barn, I noticed Gentle Jim was in his stall eating hay. When I knocked on her door and window, she did not answer and was probably in town.

Since I was frozen, I hurried into the café, expecting to see her drinking a cup of hot tea. When I asked Mrs. Potter if she had been there, she handed me a letter and said she left by train four days ago with a gentleman. My eyes fell on her words as I ripped into the envelope.

> Dear Chuck,
>
> I wish to thank you for all your kindness to me in my short stay in Powell. My decision to leave Boston was due to a great disappointment in my life. The man I was to marry said he was not ready to settle down until he saved more money. Once I left, he suddenly realized he loved me, and came to Powell to take me with him to California for a new start in life.
>
> One of my schoolmates, Alice Booth, sent a message with him that she would be taking my place here, so the school would stay open. Please be a friend to her, and goodbye.
>
> Ruth Albert

Once I was warmed up, I ate the cookhouse sandwiches on the lonely ride back to the bunkhouse. A big poker game was going on, with some beer on the table. A few eyes turned my way, and I fell on my bunk to think of my hard luck with

Ruth. When Alice Booth arrives, I decided I would dress up in my best boots and hat, so she would be impressed by her first real cowboy. Perhaps I would mention the book I just finished, and ask her if she brought any good eastern literature to read to show off my see-fist-ti-cation, as Ruth would say.

These days I'm too busy on the ranch to get much reading done now that Alice and I are married with a year-old boy and a baby girl.

Mr. Farley left the mail in the office, and Alice held up a letter and said, "Poor Ruth is coming back to Powell to teach. Her husband ran off with a dance hall girl in the saloon, and he turned out to be a gambler. She has no income and needs some help."

The thought of Ruth being back in town left me a bit weak in the knees, but I decided to give Alice Ruth's train fare. I thought I'd better forget about going into Potter's for coffee in the near future, for I did not want old memories clouding my new life.

The Campign Trip

When we first talked about going camping in the National Forest, it was just going to be Al Knapp and myself. Al mentioned our trip to a friend who told Roland Larsen, and of course, he talked himself into joining our party. We called him Rollie, and frankly he was a little bit much to take at times, and being with us for a week steady was not going to be a picnic for Al and me. His rich grandfather left him a pile of money in a trust fund so the checks would roll in every month.

When we three drove to the forest entrance, we parked our Jeep and got our gear, since we were all packing our own supplies. Of course, Rollie showed up with new everything. His top-of-the-brand hiking boots to his hunting knife and one-man tent were spanking fresh off the shelves from the camping store.

The only thing he brought that I loved was his dog Max. Rollie could afford to travel to Europe often, and the islands in the Pacific. He would let me take care of Max, and I looked forward to his company and would love to keep him. Max loved me, because Rollie had a flaw in his rich nature. He looked at Max as just a dog. Sure he fed him, but never did he pet him, play with him, talk to him, or recognize him as a companion.

He was my companion, though, because Rollie sometimes would be gone for months at a time, and Max and I would be together for that special sixty days.

We trotted up the trail, with Max at my side, and Rollie being so indifferent to just a dog never noticed he stuck with me, and it would never make him jealous for he was tuned out when it came to his dog. It was in October, and Indian Summer, so we had on long sleeve hiking shirts with all the pockets, and that kept the sun off our arms. We walked most of the day in a lazy step, but got into the tall Ponderosa Pines and set up our evening camp. We got a fire going, and cooked our beans and franks for the meal, and I fed Max since he came to me for his needs. Also, Max was a good hunter, and he could catch a squirrel, and I would skin it for him and put it over the fire for one of his snacks.

The next day we got really deep into the forest and depended on our direction by compass. Of course, Rollie had one that was super accurate, and he had to show us that our cheap ones were off a few degrees. Well, we headed up the mountain, and got to a high altitude for the night. It was a little cool there, so we had to put on light jackets, and Rollie sported his new hand knit Irish wool sweater.

When we went to bed, we each had our own sleeping bag with a nylon cover in case of rain. The high tech compass showed us the direction for the morning, but did not give out any weather reports, and some front was headed our way. When we were having breakfast, light snow began to fall, and we had to put on our nylon slickers to keep dry. By the time we packed up our gear to move on, we could hardly see a trail in the trees, and the wind was whipping a cold wind against our faces. It got so bad we had to stop and settle down under some shorter trees for a break, and we thought we had better get a fire going and stay there until it let up a bit. We found enough broken branches for firewood, but had to use a fire stick to ignite the flames since the wind was too strong to hold a match. Also we had to keep the fire in the ground, so we would not spread any flames to the trees.

The snow was now starting to mount up, and we put our sleeping bags near the coals that were almost out, but they were so deep in the hole we dug, they could not radiate heat beyond the dirt walls. By morning we hoped this front would pass through the area. I wiped the snow off Max and invited him under my nylon slicker that was over my bag, and he snuggled next to me.

By morning it was so cold in the higher altitude, we thought we should start hiking back in the direction of the car that was two days away. Getting lower out of this wind and freezing cold would be a smart move. By now we had on our warmer jackets, but still could not get warm in that biting wind. We just got in single file and started heading down with our heads low. I brought a light hood for my head, but Al had to tie an undershirt on his head to keep his ears warm. We only started with baseball caps, and they were perfect for the warm sun, but now, we had to keep our ears from freezing.

The snow was blinding, and Max was leading the way just in front of me, with Al behind me, and Rollie behind him. I thought we should take a break, and told Al to tell Rollie it was rest time. Al tapped me on the shoulder to tell me he was not there, and he must have wandered off the trail in the blinding snow. We turned to start back up the mountain a ways, and started yelling his name, but received no answer. I was pretty sure Max would scout him out with that sharp nose of his.

In the white world that had enveloped the forest, we could not see the trees five feet in front of us. Fear started creeping up my back when we could not locate him, but when Max starting barking I figured he was on his trail. We followed in the direction, until we almost reached the sound. Suddenly Max was in front of me, and would not get out of my way. As I tried to put one foot in front of me he grabbed my jacket, and held me on the spot. Then I could hear Rollie yelling for help in a very desperate way. His voice appeared to be below us, and I caught my breath when I realized I would have walked off the side of the cliff ahead of me. I felt around for a bush, hung on to it, and yelled to Rollie so he would know we were near him. Al informed him that we had no rope and could not see him in the snow. We told him to get his sleeping bag out and get it over him, and we would get him in the morning. We camped twenty feet from where I held the bush and waited for morning.

When we got up at first light, the snow was falling in very fine flakes, almost like a mist. We finally could see the treetops, so had Max lead us to the right place above the ledge. Rollie was crying and praying and asking for help, and I remembered he was afraid of heights. Now he could see the river below him, and it was a scary drop from where he was sitting. After Al tied his jacket around the base of a tree and put a strong knot in the arms, he put his feet in the loop. We told Rollie to try throwing his pack up to us, but he was so afraid of the drop under him his feeble toss just bounced off the side of the cliff wall, and the backpack sailed to the river below.

Al had a good grip on my ankles and lowered me down

as far as he could manage, with his feet anchored to the tree. Rollie was frantic and kept looking down at the water, and I had to yell at him to look up and stop crying. He kept saying, "Get me out of here, please I can't stand being here, I'll give you my older Shelby, anything you want in this world that I own. Please, please get me on solid ground."

Well, I was just a half a foot short and kept telling him to jump for my hands, but he seemed to be paralyzed by fright. I could not keep hanging there, so had Al pull me up for a rest.

Then he really started to scream, "Don't leave me here."

I reassured him we would try again, but he would have to jump that half foot to my hands.

Back in my upside down position, I started yelling at him to stop crying and begging, for we were doing the best we could, but he had to help us by jumping that extra half foot. He would not move, so Al pulled me up again for a rest. I guess I took too long, for now he was promising me the world, the car, his new camera, and so forth. I told him if he did not jump this time we would have to leave him on the ledge until we got help.

That did it, and I said, "One, two, three, jump, for God's sake."

He bent his knees ever so slowly and jumped as high as he could with a great fear of the big drop below him. No, it was not enough, and I told him we would try one more time before we would go for help. The fear of the jump was bad enough, but the thought of spending the day sitting above the cold, cold river below was the right motivation, because this time he put some spring in his shaky legs, and I was able to catch his wrists.

Now that I had him, the real work began, for I had Al pull me up slowly, but he was caught in the jacket and had to use all the muscle power he could muster in that awkward position. I was getting dizzy hanging with my head down for so long, and Rollie climbed up over my head holding my neck and waist. Somehow he was so scared he grabbed every piece of my body that would accelerate his voyage up to the top, including my legs, and then Al's arms and head. Al managed to pull me up so I could grab the bush and crawl on the snow. I stayed on my stomach for a few minutes so I could get my wind back.

As Al and I were huffing and puffing, Rollie had moved twenty feet away from the scary edge. Max licked my face as I thanked him for saving my life the night before. Now that Rollie no longer had his expensive gear from the camping store, he no longer had a load on his back and was in one big hurry to get back to the car. It was slippery going downhill, but the lower we got, the less snow there was over our boots.

We three ate some of my energy bars for lunch, which propelled us along our compass direction, and by late afternoon we finally made it near the car, since our reckoning was a bit south of it. We had to take a reading with Al's and my compass to make sure we had to turn a little north to find the parking area. That took another half hour, and we eventually made it to the Jeep. We had to put the gears in four-wheel drive to climb the slight incline, which had become slippery as the snow melted now that the sun was out. We took our time and finally made it out to the highway.

When we stopped at Rollie's house first, he said, "I am embarrassed by my yelling and crying, but my fear of heights has been with me all my life, and I can't seem to conquer it. Now I meant it when I said I would give you my Ford Shelby, and my camera, for I don't welch."

I said, "There is only one thing you own that I would want."

He was fair and said, "Just name it."

I answered "My only desire is to have Max as my own loyal dog."

He could not believe I would want just that plain old dog over his Ford Shelby.

I told him, "Max stopped me from falling over the cliff by grabbing my jacket and saved me from the river. He in turn saved you, so I was there to grab your hands."

When Rollie got out of the Jeep, Max expected to go with him, but when I said, "No Max, you stay with me now and forever," he seemed to understand and jumped next to me in the passenger seat with a big wet lick and stood to wag his tail.

With much consideration, Rollie turned around, and said, "Good dog Max, thanks," which was the only kind words Max ever heard from his lips in the five years he lived in the big house on the hill.

Max gave him a look back that said, "Too late Roland, old boy, but you had your chance."

The Housewife

My husband was a put-down artist from way back, and I spent thirty years listening to his description of my drab appearance and boring conversation. Finally he met a young chick that turned him on to a new life. Yes, I would gladly give him a divorce, for he was no love in my life after the way he treated me throughout our whole marriage. He did not want kids because they were expensive and ate up your savings, so he bought a horse instead. If you could see the feed and vet bills, you would know that he just plain did not like children, dogs, or cats, and apparently his stupid wife. Well, he was not going to give me much money, but would do the best he could. After all, he had the second mortgage on the house, plus the utilities, insurance, health care, and blah, blah, blah. I did not want the house and decided his girlfriend could dust it, vacuum, wash, and listen to him complain about his starched shirts. I gave at the office; let someone else take over the duties.

At sixty I had to hunt down a job so I could pay for my very small apartment, but it did cover my needs for a place to eat and sleep, and it was warm in the winter. Since I had no real experience except washing, ironing, dusting and cooking, I was afraid my talents were limited. A friend told me the Franklyn

Wells Auto Parts was looking for someone in the office to do simple work, like answer the phone, write a few checks and some book work.

Mr. Wells talked to me about what the job needs would require, and it seemed like I could handle it. He would let me work into it as I learned the basic routine. The other help took care of the customers, and I could sit at my own desk in the office and maybe answer the phone once in a while. My neighbor showed me how to make out checks, for I had to learn so I could pay my bills instead of running to the bank for cash, then taking it to the electric and gas company and paying my bills with real money. Now I could write paychecks in the office and found it a breeze.

Everyone was so nice to me that it was a novelty after listening to George give me grief about everything.

Keeping a record of the time the employees came into the shop was easy. When they passed my desk to hang up their coats next to Mr. Wells' office, I looked at the time and wrote it down for Mary, John, Fred, Jose, Harry, and Charlie. Sometimes one was a few minutes late, but Mr. Wells never complained about that. It was one big happy family, and I just loved working there.

George and his woman friend were hot and heavy for the beginning of their romance in my old house. I wish he had met her years ago, and I guess that was the dumb part of me, for I stayed too long at his lousy party.

George got very sick, so she decided not to be his nurse and cook anymore, thus she left him. He had to go to the hospital because he could not take care of himself and ended up with a cancer operation on his legs. He would have to get someone to clean the house when he came home, but thank God it was not his old ex-wife. Besides, he lost his job because he could not walk too well, and the factory needed a very active manager. (Goodbye wages, hello Social Security.) He did not have too much money coming in now and had to give his horse away so it would get care. As it turned out, no one wanted to buy it, and one of the fellows at the shop got tired of cleaning out the stall, brushing his hair and feeding it. Thus, George was suddenly in poor health living on less money and alone in the world.

He was somewhat better after his treatment, but he was no longer the strong, hyperactive runaround like in his old days. He tried to get work with the same company, but they had a much younger fellow in his job, and there was no place where they could use him. Did I feel sorry for him after the years of hell he gave me? No, I was now an independent working woman who could take care of herself.

Mr. Wells was a widower for twenty years and on the lonely side at times. He would take me out to lunch on occasion, and for the dumb wife of George it was a revelation to find out someone enjoyed my company. We would talk about many thing of interest, and more and more meals did we eat at the corner cafe. We went to the zoo one Sunday and had such a good time laughing at some of the animal antics that we could not remember having so much fun in years. Then a popular Broadway show was coming to the art center, so we just had to see it, plus a concert with the Philharmonic the following weekend. So life had really turned around for me. He took me to his fishing cabin on a lovely lake and showed me how to cast for trout, and I loved it. We caught enough fish between the both of us for dinner. He even cleaned and cooked them on the grill.

Life was so much fun he did not want it to end and asked me to marry him on a trip to Las Vegas. We found The Chapel Around The Corner and tied the knot on the spot. His house was twice as nice as George's and he would not let me clean it, and had a woman do it so we could be free to travel and do other things.

One day while we were parked at the post office, Franklyn was going over the mail from his large post office box. George walked by the car, and he knew my new husband, so started asking him if he had any little jobs at his store that he could do. Of course, Mr. Wells was sorry, but had more help than he needed.

Suddenly George bent below Franklyn's Cadillac window, and his eyes met mine. You could see the surprise in his expression. He said, "Is that you, Sue," and I replied "Yes." I knew my new clothes and hair perm changed my appearance so he didn't recognize me for a minute. He must have thought I was Mr. Wells' maid, and he told me he had been sick. I said, "That's too bad."

Mr. Wells informed him that I was now Mrs. Wells, and we were picking up our passports for our trip to Europe. George backed away from the car in total shock. I waved as Franklyn was about to start the car. I bent low toward the window and spoke loudly, "By the way, George, as I rate you as a husband from one to ten, you come in as a big zero."

The Inn

We were all talking about getting together for New Year's Eve and decided we would put our suggestions in a bowl and see how many of them would pick the same location for our dinner. Well, there were some good choices in the glass, but an old inn in Connecticut seemed to win by two slips of paper. It was located in a very lovely setting in the back woods, and given that there was no snow on the roads December 31st, we could all drive there without too much trouble.

On the drive up, we just had some light rain, but a cold front started to blow in once we settled down to our early evening drink around four-thirty in the afternoon.

My God, the inn was very lovely with the Christmas tree and decorations still up, plus all the pine greens picked from their own trees. We were all prepared to sleep over for the New Year's Day buffet. We were getting ready for our big New Year's Eve dinner before the champagne bottles started popping corks.

Our steaks were lovely, and they prepared baked potatoes, mashed, au gratin, and potato salad. It was fun to try a bit of each selection, plus all the nice vegetables, the asparagus, string beans, squash, coleslaw, and a glorious salad with their own blend of dressing that had the best flavor we ever tasted. We ate until we were stuffed and had to put the dessert off for an hour so our meal would settle. That left a few inches for the blueberry pie with ice cream, and it was heavenly.

After we had gorged ourselves and were happy talking and visiting, we started on the champagne, and that lasted until *Auld Lang Syne*, but frankly I did not feel too good, and Charlie said the same. By the time we all were heading for our rooms after midnight, we realized that every one of us were getting stomach cramps and feeling like up-chucking. It was a terrible night for all of us, because my wife and I had to share the john at the same time to be sick, and I had to use the trash pail.

In the morning we were too ill to even think of breakfast and stayed in the room, moaning to one another. My wife had brought some Pepto Bismol, and that helped a tad, but we were in a bad way, and I thought if I felt better in a little while, maybe I could muster up enough energy, to drive to the hospital.

Of course, by now the cold front had blown in, and so did the snow. I could see it piled high on the patio table outside our window, and surely there had to be a foot stacked on the furniture, so the road had the same amount because I never heard a plow all night. The view of the road had disappeared in the whiteness. We were sick and stranded, and when I was trying to talk to the owner about food poisoning from his meal, the phone and power went off. The storm was so thick overhead, none of the cell phones would work. The manager had sent for help in the four-wheel-drive truck, but it came back shortly with news that someone slid halfway off the bridge, and there was not enough room to pass.

I asked the manager how come they were not sick and learned that they did not eat any of the evening meal, and all had a late lunch around three-thirty, but not with our menu. Just talking about food made my stomach flip over a couple of times, and I rushed up to my room for another round of stomach purging.

By now everyone in the hotel that ingested the New Year's Eve meal was sick in their rooms. We were getting dehydrated and had to force ourselves to drink water. Since the electricity was out in the storm, we had no TV news or entertainment to get our minds off our illness. At least the gas heat in the rooms was still working, because the inn was old, and each room had its own pilot light in the iron radiator, and I used to have one in an old house. They are great, and can blast you out of the building if you turn them all up high.

As I downed more Pepto, it did seem to help the queasy feeling, and I thought maybe I could snowshoe down to the village and get some help. It was a few miles, and the wind was quite strong, but I had a ski jacket in the car, and a warm hat and gloves. By noon I felt better and could hold down the glasses of water, so my guts were well coated with the pink sauce.

My car was well covered with snow, and I had to use a rolled up newspaper to get it off the trunk to get inside for my clothes. The hotel had an old pair of snowshoes hanging on the wall in the hall, and I borrowed them and had to work at tying them on my shoes. I had no ski poles, but broke a dead branch off a nearby tree and headed for the bridge.

Sure enough, I found the car half off the bridge but crosswise with the front-end wheels hanging over the side. As I passed the windows I looked inside, and a good thing I did, for there was a little boy inside by himself. When I asked him where his father or mother was, he had some tears and told me his Mother left him inside to get help. He had slept in a heavy car quilt, so he managed to keep warm during the night. I told him maybe he should come with me, because he seemed to have warm clothes.

He was hungry, and I thought, you are lucky you missed our dinner last night. Because he had no snowshoes, he would get tired, so I had to put him on my shoulders on and off.

In my mind I had many worries, because our company was in deep trouble and the vice president was caught cheating on the books. It looked like the place could fold, and at 55 years old, I could be out on my backside. I had two car payments and a big mortgage, so lost a lot of sleep over my future. The thought that I could not land something with enough wages to carry my obligations added to my fright. Make no mistake about the word fright, for it describes it beautifully.

The first mile down the road trail was not too hard, but as I got into the second, the effort was grueling, especially with the wind. It was easy to find the road under me because it was the only opening in the woods.

As we plodded along, I tripped over something and saw a hand in the snow. My God it was a woman, and the little boy yelled, "That's my mother." Well, she was there all night long, so nothing would help her now. I dragged her to the side of the road, so the plow would not find her, and pushed the body into the side bushes.

Things were not bad enough, and now I had a sobbing boy about seven years old and had to muster up physical effort to get us both to the village. Now I had to save our own lives for it was freezing in the wind. I had to put him back on my shoulders because the snow was too deep for his little legs to move far. I thought I might have to stop and throw up, and had the feeling for about ten minutes, but it passed, as I mushed along in the high snow.

At last, we came to a part of the road that was already plowed on the other side of a big tree that had fallen across the plow's path. They needed some chain saws to clear that section to drive to the inn. The plow came down the other side of the road, pushing the deep snow off the right side. As he stopped at the tree to turn around, we yelled and flagged him. He was surprised to see us, and I told him that everyone was sick, with no power at Lyon's Inn. Also, I whispered about the boy's mother on the side of the road and her car hanging off the bridge. He told me he would take care of it. On the radio, his voice mentioned the inn and wanted the chain saw crew right away, because they were working on other trees that had fallen during the night. He drove us to the hotel where the boy and his mother were staying. His father and mother were divorced, and the boy had a card in his pocket with his father's home and office number. A doctor checked the boy and gave me something for my stomach.

The card was in my hand as I phoned the boy's father in New York. It was a business card, and I noticed he was the CEO of one of the bigger firms in the city.

I smiled when I saw the name, because Ed Scott worked for them. As a matter of fact, Ed was not one of my favorite people in our group because he made more money than most of us and was good at letting us know it by showing us his new Cadillac, or asking me about my job too frequently. My job did not pay a lot in money, and certainly I had no major title like his position, but of course that is why he was so interested.

When the boy got on the phone crying, he was telling his father about finding his mother in the snow, and I could hear his father's sad reply, but relieved his son survived in the cold car. He kept telling him, "Thank God, you are all right," and I could hear his faint voice from a few feet away.

He wanted me back on the phone and thanked me several times, and would I please come to his office in the city and meet him in person next week. Also he asked my name, and where I worked. When he heard Moore and Sons, I heard him exhale.

Everyone recovered from the food poisoning, and the plow got through to the inn, and we could manage to get back to our individual homes. As we were leaving, Ed Scott saddled up to me to tell me that he had heard about the big financial problems in my firm and left me with the parting words, "I hope you don't lose your job." Somehow I felt there was a bit of a snicker in his wish, and I had to contain my desire to punch him square on the jaw.

When I was in the city, I phoned the firm to see if the boy's father, Charles Goodwin, could see me, and he even came out to greet me. He did not shake my hand, but threw his arms around me and patted my back as he told me how grateful he was that I saved his boy from freezing. Also, he felt bad about the boy's mother, for she was a good woman and a fine mother. She had divorced him because he was too wrapped up in the business and could not be at home like the partner she wanted in life.

He said, "Let's go out to lunch," and asked me how I

liked working at Moore and Sons, and I gave him an honest answer. He knew the firm and shook his head slowly as he said, "Too bad about their problems." He mentioned that he had some inside information on the company's financial records, and that he was positive it was going to fall into bankruptcy quite soon. Also, he had checked up on my years at the firm, and what my job encompassed. He informed me that he would do anything for me, after what I did for his son, and asked me more about my qualifications in this, that, and everything, and information on my education.

Since one of their top vice presidents was about to retire, he had an open mind about getting a new man in the office. I perked up because Ed sort of bragged that he had a good shot at the job while we were eating our poison meal. I mentioned Ed's name, because I knew he worked there, and told him I just spent the New Years with the gang at the inn, and Ed Scott was in the group. He implied, in a nice way, that Ed was a bit cocky and over confident, and not his favorite, but he did hustle for the company. He just did not have leadership qualities, because he was too abrasive to other workers and not popular with the office staff.

He shook my hand and said, "I like your qualifications, and want a non-company worker for the new vice president job, and I am going to offer it to you. Any man that would walk through that deep snow with my son on his shoulders and has done such a good job at Moore and Sons for as long as you have can handle this job. I want you in the office as soon as you can sever the cord from Moore's. My spies did an extensive check up on your work ethics, and you got an A plus."

A week later at the board meeting, the men sat around

the large oval table in the plush conference room. Mr. Goodwin poured some wine from a large decanter and announced why they were all there. He said he had given the choice of vice president much thought, and he wanted what was best for the company, and had picked a fine young fellow from Moore and Sons. He opened the door, grabbed my hand, and shook it hard as he pulled me into the room. "Gentlemen, meet your new Vice President, John Grant." When my eyes met Ed Scott's, he leaned over the table and threw up.

The Secretary

Life was good now that we finally had our own house after renting apartments for ten years. Tommy just got on the school bus, and Clay went to his insurance business at seven-thirty. He and his partner, Ted Beacham, were now making money and made some good deals with a few local business establishments. All of the workers got a discount for their autos and houses in a package at our insurance company. With more than a hundred and fifty of them paying by the month instead of the usual six-month payment, the money rolled in every thirty days. Besides, they had other customers that contributed to their income.

Before we were married, Clay wanted to buy me a diamond engagement ring, but we decided to save the money for a good down payment on a house. Of course, I missed having one to show off to my girlfriends, but money in the bank was more important, because Clay said he wanted half of the price of a house for a down payment on a mortgage, so the other half could be paid off in fifteen years.

Doing my dishes, washing clothes, and cleaning made me a happy housewife now that it was my own home. I just would play music on the radio and dust the furniture with a song in my heart. Sometimes I would work in the flowerbeds in the late afternoon and water the lawn. The place looked very presentable with my little touches, and it made our Cape Cod house attractive to the neighborhood.

The phone rang, and it was Clay. He asked me to meet him at the Hillside Hotel for lunch, since he was taking a long break before meeting with a client. This seldom ever happened, so I did my hair and picked out a nice outfit to show off. When I looked in the mirror, I looked quite presentable and still weighed about the same weight as the day we were married. Some of my girlfriends had turned a bit beefy in the past number of years, so I guess I felt a little smug.

Clay was at the dining table ahead of me and handed me the menu. He ordered the steak, and the choice of shrimp appealed to my taste buds as I felt like seafood today. When I was into my second bite of ice cream, my husband hesitated while he cleared his throat and wiped me out with, "I want a divorce, Helen."

When I looked up to his cold face I knew it was no joke. The shock had tears flooding my vision, and I stumbled out past glares from strange faces as my sobs hit an audible decimal.

Once home, Clay came barging into the bedroom saying he was sorry, but he had fallen in love with their new secretary who was a lovely young beautiful girl. He never meant to hurt me, and it just seemed to happen as time flew by.

I could keep the house, and everything financially would be the same, as he would continue to pay the usual bills and send me a check for expenses such as food, clothing and money for Tommy.

Time moved along very slowly after the divorce, and

Clay's partner told me Clay married two days after the final papers were received. Such sadness and misery hit me like a ton of bricks, and I spent too many nights crying myself to sleep. Up until Clay met this very young gal, he seemed content and happy with our marriage. I had to get on with my life and took some courses at night school to improve my typing and computer skills. Tommy would stay with the baby sitter these nights, but still had not adjusted to being without a father at the end of day.

Clay's partner would come by on occasion to check on us, and would throw the baseball with Tommy in the backyard. His wife was in a mental hospital for fifteen years after losing a two-month-old baby boy. She just never seemed to come out of the shock of her loss. I guess Tommy filled some void in his sorrow and lonely life, and Ted would bring him bats and baseballs for his Little League activities. He was much older than Clay, and he was a very decent person and good influence on my son.

Clay seemed to avoid Tommy, probably because he felt guilt for his actions. So he just stayed away from us. It hurt the boy because his lack of visits made him think he drove his father from our house. It put responsibility on me, for I had to try to explain that his father met a woman that stole his love from me and it had nothing to do with his father's love for him.

Clay's partner showed up at ten in the morning while I was having another cup of coffee. Needless to say, I was surprised because it was an unusual time for a visit. He pussyfooted around the bush until he blurted out that Clay was in an accident driving to work on his long commute from his new home in Newport. It was twenty-five miles from the office, and he made a left turn on a caution light as a bus was coming straight down the road. It slammed into the passenger side of the car, folding it like an accordion. The doctors thought he was killed instantly. Of course, I felt terrible for Clay, and Tommy would be sick over the loss of his father. I supposed his new wife would now get most of his income, and I was going to lose the payments on the house, plus our income. What about our plans for sending Tommy to college in eight years, for this would take money.

After the grief and depressed emotions settled down, Ted had coffee with me one day and had to explain, "Clay's supposed wife went after him big time throwing herself at him with every trick in the books. I suppose he tried to ignore it at first, but her campaign was a big attack, since she fell all over the poor man with her sexy dress and deportment. As it turns out, she was still married and separated from a commercial seaman. Therefore, you were still his legal wife all this time. Thus, you will get the big insurance settlement, which I personally wrote up for him the day we signed our partnership. You won't lose the house, and there is also enough for Tommy's college fund. She spent so much money, he sold out his partnership to me in despair. Maybe you could fill in at the office, since I fired her right after they were married, and I have been trying to run most of the whole show myself."

When I came to work, he showed me the books, and I just had to put the amount of payment after the people's names so we could know who was keeping up with their car and house insurance installments. He gave me some lessons in policies and general bookkeeping, and I found the work interesting.

The office door flew open, and Clay's supposed wife started yelling at Ted and demanded Clay's half of the business money. He had to inform her that her spending forced Clay to liquidate his half of the business to pay for her many luxury items, like the new car, house, washer, dryer, furs and jewelry. Also, the lawyer had exposed the fact that she was still legally married to a merchant marine seaman named, Arthur Green, and bigamy is against the law.

I walked into Ted's office, since I could hear every word through the open door, and slapped her across the face with gusto, announcing that she cheated my son out of a father. Then I slapped the powdered and rouged face again with my hundred and thirty pounds behind it. This knocked her back off her feet, and I quickly bent over her and grabbed the diamond ring off her finger.

She screamed, "You thief, I'll have you arrested."

I replied, "Will this be before or after you are arrested for bigamy? Clay and I were still married, so this is my money, and my engagement ring. Better yet, why don't you just sue me, Mrs. Green, and don't forget to pay the bank for your house mortgage, the car dealership, for your new car, the Sears store for the washer, dryer, the fur store for the mink coat, and the jewelry store for the diamond ring. Since you bought the ring, the store will want it returned if the payments don't arrive on time each month. If you tell them I have it, I will deny it."

Mrs. Green turned to Ted and said, "you saw her take the diamond off my finger?"

Ted looked at her with a surprised look and replied, "Madam Green, you do suffer from delusions. What diamond ring?"

Water-Logged

When my friends the Thompsons, Jean and Ray, invited me on their new sailboat for the weekend, I hesitated. First of all, they always had their neighbors with them, Sara and Ross Glynn. The four of them put down booze like baby's milk. Ross was an obnoxious tease, especially when he was doing his favorite thing, drinking vodka.

Though I was always a strong swimmer, getting pinned under the keel of a sailboat in the sand took the edge off the ocean. We were just diving off the deck one day in calm waters and going under the keel and coming up the other side for a lark, when the keel pinned me. I had to frantically dig in the sand to free myself, and it was an effort to escape. Never did I do that stunt again, and my respect for the water produced a slight fear that I could not seem to shake off.

Jean invited me because we were good friends, but also felt sorry for me because her brother and I just broke up after a long engagement. Under pressure from her, I relented and grabbed a book, camera and some sunscreen. True to form, the beer, scotch and vodka flowed like Niagara, so I moved to the bow and gave everyone a wide berth. Frankly, I was never a good sailor due to an inner ear problem, but as long as the water was on the calm side, my nausea was under control.

Ross gave me the usual hard time and made fun of me sitting in leisure encased in my life jacket, but it was not that uncomfortable and added peace of mind to my insecurity.

Jean always had tons of good food, so when we got a few miles away from shore, the gang decided to have a swim before lunch. Ray turned the motor off and glided to a calm spot, and I was prepared to stay in place and read my new book. Ross started pestering me to join them and live a little, but I gave him a loud NO, and he made fun of me in his familiar style. Finally I gave him the finger and told him to get lost. Always, this got a big laugh out of him, but I learned not to put up with his pain in the neck antics.

They sure looked slightly intoxicated already as they hit the water. Everyone took a dive, jump, or just slipped overboard. Sara used the ladder to ease her two hundred pounds into the water. They certainly were having a grand time laughing and bobbing around the boat. Ross was saying he would be the first to the buffet and reached up to the ladder and lifted it straight in the air, which unlocked the two hooks that held it to the side of the boat. He floated with it for control, because no one could board without it.

As I ignored their frolicking, I sank deeper into my book and got lost in the story. Once in a while a little swell would sway under me, lifting and pitching the deck a bit. As I looked up I scanned the horizon and could see a lightning flash in the very distant clouds. Some big wave rolled the boat, the winds began to pick up, and it looked like the storm was headed in our direction.

I heard Ray yell at Ross because the ladder had drifted

away while he was horsing around with his wife. It had moved faster than he expected, and he started swimming after it with his portly frame bucking some small waves. He was losing ground, and he was now so far away that Sara was yelling at him to come back. By now, I was on my feet and he was having a hard time paddling in the swells.

A bit of a panic was setting in, as no one could board, and now they were all aware of the impending storm. I tried to lift the anchor to throw it overboard, but Ray used overkill in his choice of chain and anchor, for I could not lift it. Finally I tied bed sheets together, added knots every few feet, and hung it over the side after I tied it to the rail. Ray came aboard, hand over hand, so he could help Jean and Sara on deck. Jean flew up the knots, but Sara could not pull her beef past the second knot. Ray told her to just hang on while he went after Ross who was in a current quite a distance from us by now. He seemed to be laboring against the waves.

Once the engine was fired up, we slowly went on a course to Ross, and picked him up. Then he and Ray could help Sara board by both getting her up high enough to grab her hands. The panic seemed to be over, and out came the drinks again, so life was back to normal. Since the storm was still miles away, the food started coming out, and they would relax and recover and enjoy Jean's lunch before heading for shore.

They drank and ate for a half hour and were having a great time by the joking and singing that floated up from the cabin. Ross came up with some oysters when Jean mentioned I could not eat and felt a touch of seasickness. He started describing all the dishes to my queasy stomach, greasy bacon, potato salad and raw oysters. My stomach almost came up in my throat, but I would not give him the satisfaction of barfing. Finally, I told him to go stuff himself, and of course he did not want to miss another drink, so did his laugh and departed.

When I looked up, I could see this tremendous wave headed in our direction and, frankly, it took my breath away when I saw its size. I gave an earth-shattering yell that brought them up the stairs, and the next thing I knew I was in the water with Jean. Ross was yelling for Sara, and Jean was screaming for Ray.

I was the only one in a life jacket, so had no trouble floating near all the debris and boat gear. Ray appeared next to Jean from nowhere, saying, "Thank God, you are all right." Ross was hanging on to a deck chair still yelling for Sara, but his efforts were in vain, for she had vanished. When the boat tipped, it took on water quickly and could not right itself, and I remembered that everyone was on deck except Sara. I presumed she never got up the steps to the deck and was trapped in the cabin.

We floated in the dark with rain pelting our heads and terrifying lightning crashing in our ears above us. The lightning flashes gave us a view of one another, like being caught in a flash bulb for that one-second exposure.

By morning, the sea was again calm, and by the first light of morning illuminated our situation. I found myself alone floating on the support of the jacket. I not only worried about my survival, but wondered if the others were all right some place out of my sight.

Coast Guard boats were working overtime looking for survivors, because many sail boats got flipped on their sides by the same wave. It certainly happened that way with Ray's new expired schooner, but I'm sure that was the least worry by any of us, if we were all still alive.

Other crafts were also searching, and a cruiser pulled alongside me. When I reached up for help, I heard Jean call my name. Ray was by her side on deck and looked terrible, like he was in a state of shock. He whispered to me that Ross drifted away crying for Sara, and told him he did not want to live without her. Ray could not restrain his will power, and he just swam into the darkness.

Our sea tragedy was so painful that it affected our friendship, and Jean and I drifted apart, for I think down deep they felt responsible in some way for Sara and Ross. Perhaps if we had headed right to shore when we noticed the distant storm, that would have given us enough time to escape the big wave, but who expected that freak thing to develop and sweep our way.

My proximity to the ocean no longer appealed to me, and I decided to move out west to be near the mountains and try a whole new world away from any coastline. It seemed to give me a secure, peaceful environment, and also presented me with a deep pleasure, since I could watch the morning sun break on the mountain crest when I stepped out of bed, and it presented an evening sunset reflection with a yellow glow as the day ended. The real draw was the fact that I would never have to wear another life jacket for the rest of my life, never, never, never, amen.

Wyoming Days

Mr. Howell sent Josh and me to the northern border of the ranch to pick up some strays the hands missed in the fall roundup. Times were tough, so we were only temporary help until November. They had a fair corral that needed fixing, so we brought the team and wagon with some extra fence posts and cross rails. When we rode the bushes scouting for loose cows and calves, we put the team in the corral and fetched them water from the nearby windmill tank.

The late October morning was cool on our backs, but by noon the sun had warmed the air. We ran four cows and three calves to our patched corral and made some coffee and beans and salt pork for our meal.

By afternoon, we chased five more Herefords through the gate, checked the water, and put out cut grass from our supply. As the temperature dropped, the wind came up, so we had to shield our dry grass and leaves to start the fire. We managed to ignite it after ten matches and quickly added some old branches so we could heat some food.

Once the coffee cups were rinsed, we decided to cover the saddles and personal gear with the wagon tarp. The wind filled it out like a sail, as we tried to pull it over the wagon bed and make a tent enclosure for our bedrolls. We had to stake the ends into the ground so they would not flap and keep us awake.

In the early morning, we were in a full force blizzard and had to wrap our blankets and canvas cover around us to keep warm. Since we could not cook, we ate bites of cold food during the day. We checked the animals and water, and their backs faced the wind with their heads bowed low. They seemed to be holding up, so we crawled back into our sheltered nest. After the second day, we had a white tent due to the drifts that stacked up against the canvas tarp. Our bedrolls were most welcome in the gusts that rattled the wagon.

When the snow stopped falling, the wind blew the dry ground snow in white outs, so it was impossible to see the horses and cattle, but we were afraid to walk outside for fear of getting lost if we missed the fence. We sat out the day trying to keep warm wrapped in our bedding. It gave us time to talk over the howling wind about our desire for a warm meal, and the upcoming move to Josh's brother's spread near Eagle Nest, New Mexico. He had a small cabin we could use on his two-hundred-acre spread. We would feed the calves to fatten them for the market, plus take care of the pigs and turkeys.

As soon as we could collect the few more strays, we would drive them to the horse corral at headquarters. There they would separate the calves from the mothers and put the cows with the two hundred head of Herefords to be shipped to the Kansas City stockyard.

It was a hard ride back to the ranch pushing our bunch because of the snow, and the calves slowed us down with their short legs. They stuck close to their mothers, and we drove forward toward the ranch. Finally, we ran them in the horse enclosure and gave them some fresh hay and water. We had to leave the wagon in the drift, and a cowboy would have to drive it out when the snow melted in a few weeks.

The women at the cook house made us some fresh coffee, with a plate of stew, so we were content to eat and find our warm bunks.

Since we were all packed with fresh wages in our pockets, it was time to say goodbye to the hands at breakfast. We would miss them all, and the good poker games and jokes. We felt smug, rubbing it in that we were leaving the Wyoming winters and heading south. We promised them some post cards, and they said don't forget to write.

It took us a week to cross the New Mexico border towing the horse trailer and camping along the way. In the morning, we would be at Josh's brother's ranch. We parked in some open field, let the horses out to graze, and hobbled them near the truck. We cooked a fair meal, sat drinking coffee, and thinking about our new life.

At four in the morning, the wind and snow were so strong it woke us up, and by daybreak there were six inches of snow on our bedrolls. We had to use tree branches under the back wheels for enough friction to move the Ford truck to the road in low gear. We crept along the back road, with the windshield wipers slapping us a clouded view through the glass.

Josh had written five cards for the boys, and one was a bright New Mexico sunset with a red sky. He rolled the window down and tossed them into the strong wind. Because of the cold air, I turned just in time to see the bright sunset lift in the wet flakes. He rolled the window up and said, "Welcome to the Southwest," and gave a loud sigh.

Cheap Ransom

A bad joke had been played on me, as well as my kidnapers. The Stewarts had the brokerage, banking and largest car company in town. Also, they owned the biggest house on the hill overlooking their small kingdom. Because I sometimes used my maiden name, Stewart, someone impressed these three youths that I was Joseph Stewart's daughter. My father was a dirt farmer from Nebraska and had expired when he got bit by a rattlesnake as he forked hay in the barn, and that was ten years ago.

They told me they had tried to save enough money to buy a new car and drive to California. They wanted to go to Hollywood with some money for an apartment and some nice clothes. They were star struck, having been in the dramatic club at high school. It was Hollywood or bust.

Their manual jobs did not pay enough for their expensive plans, thus some cash for ransom came to mind. I tried to convince them that they had the wrong Stewart, but they told me it was a good try, since they knew I was the only daughter of moneybags Stewart.

Now remember, I was dealing with three 19-year-old disillusioned fools. On hearsay, they teamed me up to the

Stewart's money. My husband worked for a plumbing outfit, and all he could muster in ransom would be a new toilet and bathroom sink.

To say that they were ignorant was to be kind. They were stupid is more the right phrase. Not one of them ever checked to see who I really was in town, and when I tried to spell it out, it rolled off their backs. They would not tell me what idiot passed on this ridiculous falsehood.

Well, we ended up in an old farmhouse, and it seemed one of the boys was house sitting for his uncle while he was visiting part of the family in Ireland. They had the house for a month and intended to be on their way to California in a week or so.

When I asked them how much ransom they were asking, one hundred thousand was the reply. No million dollars from a rich Stewart, I asked? Well, they were not really dishonest, and really only wanted enough for the new Mustang and cash for their needs.

In the back of my mind, I seemed to remember that there was a Stewart daughter, but my memory told me she had died in a car accident in college. I don't think her name was Ruth like mine, but maybe so.

One of the boys cooked meals for the four of us and bragged that he cooked in a diner for six months. No diner could produce what we were eating. When I pressured him for some recipes, he confessed he mostly flipped burgers. I sent them off to the store for spaghetti, Italian sausage, tomato sauce, and enough goods for my favorite meatballs. They were a hit, so I took over the cooking.

When I saw the ransom note done the way they did

it in the old movies, I smiled to myself. They had cut out the letters from a magazine and used white glue to stick them down. WE HAVE YOUR DAUGHTER - WANT ONE HUNDRED THOUSAND DOLLARS FOR HER RETURN - WILL CONTACT YOU. No rubber gloves were used, and you can only guess how many fingerprints in glue it contained.

They called themselves A, B, and C so I would not know their names. B was going to drive his real old VW to the post office and mail the note. Since my purse had a fistful of bills to mail, I asked B to drop them in the box with his note.

I was guessing that they might use their cell phone for the call, but was surprised that they knew of a pay phone in the local hotel. Can you imagine what a shock was in store for Mr. Stewart when he was told they had his daughter, for he would surely ask if it was a sick joke after he told them she had died in a car accident.

When B came back from his mission, he repeated what I had told them about the car accident. Now they were going to kill their friend, Jeff, because he convinced them I was the offspring of said Stewart. One of the boys started crying only because he wanted to go to California so badly.

Well, let's face it, they were stuck with me. I figured I should suggest robbing a bank or store and letting me take leave of the folly. No, they wanted to keep me a little longer to cook while they had time to think. I baked some brownies and chocolate chip cookies, and made meat loaf, mashed potatoes, and coleslaw.

One boy had to go home for his mother's birthday, and we watched the movie, *Meet Me In St. Louis*. I asked if they considered taking the bus to LA and having a garage sale so they could sell off their expensive toys. They started saying the value of their I-pods, cameras, stacks of CDs, and one motorcycle, and they were overjoyed that someone had come up with a money plan.

I told them I would throw in two old bicycles and a lawn mower if they would take me home. When they found the ransom note and my electric bill had ended up between the passenger seat and door on a left turn, they offered to take me home. C put me on the back seat of his Harley and took me to my front door. He said he would be back with his friend's truck on Saturday to pick up the mower and bikes. Would I mind writing down my meatball recipe for his mother?

When I walked in the kitchen, my husband rushed up to me apologizing for the way he talked to me when we had our argument the day the boys took me to the farmhouse. I told him I got mad and needed a vacation. He begged me to forgive him and swore he would not lose his temper again, and please swear you'll never walk out on me again. I told him I missed him too, and loved him very much. Frankly, I almost forgot we had the argument. Also I added, by the way, you don't have to take the old lawn mower and two bicycles to the dump. I donated them to charity.

The Four Corners Country Store

When my husband went out for cigarettes, the two kids and I went to bed. I figured he was in one of his favorite haunts drinking beer with the boys, and I felt my irritation rise. As a husband, he was a flop; and as a father, his indifference to the kids was obvious.

By morning, he would reek of alcohol and be asleep on the couch. At breakfast, he was not in the living room, so I supposed he went directly to work after a night of carousing with his pals.

When I put the roast in the oven for dinner, I had added the extra potatoes he liked with the gravy. By six, he usually came in the door as hungry as a wolf. By seven, the kids and I ate, for the roast was out of the oven and cool by then.

At eight thirty, I phoned one of his friends at work, only to learn he did not show up at the garage. Rumor had it one of the big slot machines paid off at the casino, and he and John Rogers had all kinds of cash. It seems they were headed for Miami and the Bahamas. He left me with eighty dollars in the kitchen jar, plus my old broken down Ford and a pile of bills for electricity, gas and rent.

Would he be home in a week? I had my doubts, for he

loved to drink and gamble. After four weeks, we had to move, for the rent was overdue. We had survived on dry rice, beans and frozen hot dogs and pretty much what was left in the larder.

We packed our clothes, some blankets, and headed out of town toward a more populated location where I could find work. As I saw the town disappear in my rearview mirror, a sinking feeling hit me with the responsibility of my two kids depending on me alone. The shop where Al worked only restored autos for resale in California, and with all his faults, he was a top man on engines and bodywork. We just got by, but had enough for the basic things in food, heat, and a roof over our heads.

We bought a loaf of bread with a small bottle of mustard, baloney, and slices of cheese for our sandwiches, and downed them by the side of the road. We shared a bottle of milk in three plastic cups.

When we had to fill the tank, I pulled into a store with some gas pumps on the side of the building. With no one to help me, I entered the quaint store. It was a country affair with everything from shoes, shirts, pants and groceries. The man complained that the gas attendant just took off for Oregon and left him high and dry. I jumped at the chance to pump his gas and do some chores around the place. He smiled and reminded me that I was a woman. I then added, yes, a woman alone with two kids and no place to live. His face lit up in surprise, and I could see him thinking. Finally he suggested I look at the apartment above the garage in the back and see if I could manage there until we decided how this would work out. The attendant that just left was a neat person, so maybe there would be no mess to greet us.

It was fine, with two small bedrooms, a clean bath, and kitchen, plus the living room. Because it was cold outside, the kids tried the television, and it came right on with a good picture. The owner had given them each a bag of popcorn, so they were content and happy. When I talked to him, he mentioned a fair salary, and he would throw in some food from his small grocery section. We were very lucky to land there the day his helper departed.

He ran the store with his son, Jack, and a couple of young boys that stocked food items. As soon as the bell rang, I would head out the door and pump gas by the dollar amount. Most customers said ten dollars regular, twenty dollars high test, so the bills were pretty much handed to me in the amount stated. I knew how to use the old cash register, since I used to use one in a five and ten cent store before I was married. It was a break not to have to deal with the new computerized model.

We started out with rain, which turned to snow, and I was offered a pair of gloves. I talked to the many customers with a big smile, and they were surprised to see a woman handle the gas hose. Being friendly did not hurt, for some of them offered me tips when I was finished. I had nine dollars when we closed at six. The kids were thrilled when I gave them each a dollar to spend in the store the next morning. Can you imagine how happy I was to not sleep in the car with two kids and no bathroom? I really lucked out to run low on gas when we rolled into the Four Corners Country Store. The gas registered the gallons and cash amount in the store, and when I turned in the money, it was to the penny. He was pleased I was friendly with the locals, since he knew most of them by their first names. The fact that I received tips made him happy because I received more in one day than the other gas jockey made in a month.

The next morning the man introduced me to his son, Jack Junior, and he was about eight years older than I. He later told me about the small school over the hill, and he covered the pumps for me while I registered both my daughter and son on the spot. They said all the kids were friendly, and the teacher had them all say welcome to Greg and Margaret Baker, and to the town of Hillsford.

We were two hundred miles from our old house, so imagine my surprise to see someone I knew at the gas pump. She looked more than shocked to see me and had attended a church convention fifty miles north of here. She could hardly wait to tell me that Al had come back to the vacated house looking for us. He finally spent all the money on booze and gambling, so was now broke. The auto shop hired someone else, so he had no money, no job, no house, and was living in his truck. I begged her not to mention seeing me, but I knew she was a blabbermouth.

Jack Junior was very nice to my kids and went out of his way to be friendly and polite to me. Sometimes we would eat a quick lunch together in the station during a slow period so we could visit. His wife and baby were killed by a drunk driver, and he was just starting to cope with it after six months. He thought he was on top of his grief now and seemed to be a happier person. When he asked me to the movies, he wanted the kids too, so we were having a bit of fun driving to the next bigger town singing "Old McDonald Had A Farm," which the kids liked. All of us were laughing, and we had adjusted to our new situation and ate together in a nice restaurant more happy than we thought possible.

Both kids never mentioned their dad, and I understood why, for he had ignored their needs as a father figure all their short lives. Jack and I started really dating because we sometimes left the kids with his widowed father so they could play Monopoly with him. Jack knew I was married, and we discussed a divorce on desertion. He was lining me up a lawyer next week.

My worst nightmare came to town and demanded to see his wife and kids. Jack and I were eating lunch in the office at the pumps when I saw him go in the store. When I went to the door, he was threatening to take the kids, and I was glad they were in school.

It got so bad, Jack called the police and arranged for me to sign a restraining order. When the kids heard their father had arrived, they were shaking, and so was their mother. I guess they were afraid we would have to move back home again.

At night, we locked the doors and crossed our fingers. Unbeknown to me, he was already in the apartment sleeping in a closet, and I got a whiff of alcohol when I walked near it. He jumped out of the door with the gun in his hand, grabbed me by the neck, and put the pistol to my head. It was a cold piece of metal, and I remembered that he always had it in his truck.

He was raving that he owned us and could kill me and the kids because we ran out on him. When I explained he had left me without funds for food, gas, electricity, and rent, it fell on deft drunk ears. He threw me on the bed, and the kids coward in the corner of the room. Well, I was so scared I was heaving in a flowerpot, and he kept the three of us locked in the bedroom all of the night. I wondered what would happen in the morning when I did not show up for work. I was scared for myself, but petrified because of the danger to Margaret and Greg.

At ten AM, Jack guessed we were locked upstairs, since the kids did not pass on their way to school. He had the police there in jig time, and they paged Al on the loud speaker and told him to come out with his hands up. Now he was really mad, cussing at me and the world, and scaring the kids as they clung together and cried. He was telling them to shut up as he shot a few bullets out of the bedroom window and hit the police car. I could hear them coming up the stairs and kicking in the door. I figured he would kill us before they got in.

Greg made the mistake of yelling his hate at Al, and I saw him raise the gun and fire. Greg folded on his knees, and then on his face. Margaret was screaming, and I was crying and yelling as I put my arms around Greg. He was about to shoot me when I heard a click, and the gun had jammed. A loud pistol shot from the police knocked him backward against the wall. As he slowly slid on the floor, I could see blood flow through his teeth, so I knew he was dead.

Jack carried Greg to his truck and raced to the hospital ten miles away. The police followed with Margaret and me, and she seemed to be in shock from the ordeal. The doctor gave her pills to make her sleep, and I joined her with a valium to make me relax, but only after I knew Greg was going to be all right.

Jack was by my side and held my hand. It felt so good to have someone care and feel your agony. Never in my life did I ever experience that loving touch. It gave me an anchor for my floundering ship, and I felt at last that life had some happiness for my little family in the four corners of the world.

California Bound

We were going to take a trip from New York to California. We each had to throw a hundred dollars in the pot for expenses. With the four of us, that would be four hundred dollars a day for food, gas, and a motel for all of us. We would draw a piece of paper out of a hat, and two of them would say bed on them. The two that got the zero on the page had to sleep on the floor in their sleeping bags. The car was an old Ford sedan, and we had to chip in for brakes and tires before we departed. The first day out, we did quite well and ate like kings, filling the tank without any effort, and landing in a big motel room. I ended up with a twin bed, and Pete offered me ten bucks to sleep on it facing upside down for shoulder room. I declined, for I wanted to sleep alone, since another body turning and tossing would compromise my sleep.

After breakfast at McDonald's we still had some cash in the kitty. By noon before lunch we went into our collection phase, and Pete only came up with a fifty dollar bill. This did not go over at all, so we started giving him a hard time because we were only one day on the road, and we found ourselves with a deadbeat. How much money did he have, and what was he going to throw in the wallet in the morning? He was on burgers while we ate in restaurants, and he would get no pity from us. When we all put our money in the care of George, he put it in a small wallet that was kept apart from his own money. He was an honest Abe, so he was our first choice to trust with our meal ticket. In fact, we made everyone pay up front to him to make sure no more cheapskates were going to hold off on their share. Pete only came up with four hundred dollars for the whole trip. He was going to have to make cheese sandwiches from the quick stop stores, for he was off our restaurant list.

The second and third day we saw some beautiful country off the interstates, and personally, I enjoyed seeing the little towns in middle America. We stopped at a motel, and there was a bookstore in the mall near it, so we went in there to look around and found a game room next to it. Thus, we stayed for a few hours playing every machine, and liking it.

Because Pete did not pay his full share, we did not let him put his name in the hat for a bed and banished him to his sleeping bag on the floor.

We found a Denney's for breakfast and had their grand slam breakfast for three, except Pete. When George went to pay the bill, he could not find his little blue wallet. We sucked in air and wondered about all the guys crowding around us at the games last night, and I remember being pushed a bit. Oh boy, we had just about all our cash inside it and wondered if we could make California after all. To say we were in the dumps would be a gross understatement, for we hit low tide.

We thought the only thing we could do now was look around town and see if we could find a job to build up cash for the rest of the trip. Four paychecks would mount up in jig time, and we could continue our trek west. We bought the evening paper and looked through the jobs. They needed a helper in a school to clean johns and mop floors with so much pay an hour. The regular custodian was in the hospital for an operation. That appealed to Pete, so he got first and only choice on that one. A male barber was another one that caught Ray's eye, for he said he had some training and could do a regular man's haircut because he did many when he was in the service. I was interested in the job at the bank, because I had worked as a teller for five years. George was a free spirit, borrowed the money from his parents for the trip, and thought he could run the projector at a new theater, since he had done that part time when in high school.

The following morning we all went to the places we had mentioned, and everyone picked up the job except George. They wanted to make sure he was going to stay and work, and he made the mistake of saying he was on his way to California. Yes, George was honest like our first president, but dumb like some of the later White House heads.

We all came back tired, but happy to know that in a few weeks' pay, we could resume our journey. Some guilt came with it, because we were not being fair to our jobs by leaving for San Diego as soon as we had cash.

My job at the bank was the usual, cashing checks and doing accounts. The office had checked the bank back home, and my recommendations were fine, so security passed me without any reservations.

At the end of the week, a strange man came to my window, and when I looked in his face, I thought I saw a fake mustache and a wig. This gave me a chill, and wham, there was the note on the counter asking for money or take a bullet in the stomach. Since that was all he could hit through the lower cage below the glass, I did a stupid thing. I dropped to the floor and crawled along the front of the partition, and he could not get his gun down low enough to shoot or even see me. I started yelling and people started running out the door. Not too smart, for now the only people left in the bank were lying on the floor with a gun pointed toward them. He was saying, you better pass out some cash now, or these people depart this world.

The woman teller next to my cage was scared stiff and started throwing money on the floor, and it was landing all over the tile. She was a bit cheap and had tossed tens and twenties, and of course he wanted fifties and hundreds. When he shook his gun at her, hundreds came out of her drawer in heaps. Of course, he had to pick it up, so goofy me came charging out of my position and jumped on him as he was dropping the money so he could brace himself for a shot. Luckily, I was Jack be nimble, and Jack be quick, and get your fanny on him pronto. I nailed him to the floor and got the gun away after I got his arm back out of firing aim. He socked me a hard blow and tried to regain the gun, but my soccer leg gave him one quick shot in the chandelier, so he was like a lamb holding his groin and moaning.

By then, the police were in the lobby dragging him out the door. Some of the customers were picking up the money until the police said, leave it there, for we will take care of it.

The bank robber had a long record and was on the TV program that listed the most wanted ten men. Ha, he had a reward on his head, and number one boy was in line for five thousand dollars, but it would take a few weeks to get it. My name got in the paper, so I could not hide my financial expectations from the gang.

They all wanted to quit their respective jobs the next day, but I said, no way, for you're still going to put money in the kitty, and that goes for me too. The time dragged on, and they seemed to use some of their money for the motel room and meals, and saved the rest for the road. Just driving around town after work finding new places to eat, our car started sounding sick. It groaned and moaned, so it was off to the Ford dealer. They kept it for two days and announced that we needed a new transmission. I could see my five thousand evaporating before my eyes. They said it would take two thousand for parts and labor. We thought of buying another used car, but then we were afraid we would end up with some other people's bad transmission, so once it was fixed we would know what we were getting. The tires and brakes were new, so we sprung for it. No, let me clarify that I sprung for it, though I still did not have the money. They had the car and two hundred dollars, so had collateral.

Back to work we went, and our trip was being pushed back each day. We had to leave the car there for longer than expected, since they were waiting for parts. George did not like his job and quit, and just had enough money to take the bus home, thus he departed us. Pete's father was on the phone, telling him to stop wasting his time and come home and get a job. The pressure was too much, and when his father sent him a plane ticket, he was forced to take to the air. That left the two of us, and a sick car, with less money coming in. The federal agents were now saying it would take six months for the reward, and would I give them my home address so they could send it.

This was not looking good, and the money was quite shallow for California. We hung on for a few more weeks and had to shell out our saved money for the transmission, so we were not far ahead. I brushed my teeth with caution, hoping I would not need a tooth fixed or some appendix operation. I was thinking I might have to spend the rest of my life at the bank. A break came our way. The police chief came in the bank and gave me an envelope with a check for seven thousand dollars. The old crook was worth more than they expected.

Ray and I took the money and ran. We drove to the coast in grand style with good food, and money left over after paying for the transmission. The engine never ran so good, since the gears just slid into the proper slot, and sang down the road.

When we got to the Golden State, we found a little furnished motel apartment with a small kitchen arrangement, and took in the San Diego Zoo, which was really fun. At lunch we met a couple of fellows on their lunch break that talked to us about all the good deals in travel with a nice room and car. We went back to their office with them, and it was too good to turn down when we heard the price. We were signed up and on the long flight to Honolulu.

We were anxious to see the islands and soak in the beautiful climate. The fellow at our motel told us his friend flew some store items to Molokai and he always had two extra seats, so for fifty bucks each, we could fly over for a day, get the motel near the airport, and then fly back with him. We just could not pass it up. Upon landing, it was a different world than Oahu. More like the nineteen forties in looks. We had a good meal and took a short taxi ride around our side of the island, and I remembered the stories of Father Damian and the lepers, never guessing I would ever be here.

In the morning, our pilot cranked up the engines, and

we were heading back to take a tour of Maui. In the middle of the ocean, the engine started making funny noises, and our hearts were in our throats as the prop stopped cold. We were low over the water because he wanted us to see the whales swimming together through the waves. We were about to join them, and we put pillows in front of our faces as we hit the water. The plane floated long enough for us to get out with our Mae West vests around our shoulders, but the water was rough and we tried not to get a mouth full of salt water each time we bobbed up and down. Getting out of the plane door was the hardest thing my muscles ever had to do, because some part of my clothing was caught, and it was about to pull me down with the fuselage. Finally, I ripped some article of material, and it set me free. I came up gasping and trying to avoid a mouthful of water. Ray got out first and was ten feet from me, and the pilot was tying a little strap to him so he would not drift off. He yelled to me to come over to him, and he tied me to Ray.

It was still morning, and I wondered if he got a radio message off to the tower in Molokai. He did not answer me, so that told me it was, no. We rolled around all night, and I tried not to think of sharks, but knew they were out there. In the morning, I saw a fin glide by, but it disappeared. A plane was flying in low over us, and I guessed Honolulu missed our return flight after they talked to the Molokai tower. They dipped their wings, and a short time later a helicopter dropped a rubber raft. We had to swim for it, but had little strength to pull our weight into it. The craft hovered over us, and finally they had someone jump in the sea to assist us. One by one, we rose over the waves and soon were all back in Honolulu, safe from the sharks and foam.

We visited Maui for a week, with the prearranged motel for our headquarters.

Ray announced to me that he was going to stay and not go back to the mainland. He loved the land and the climate, and thought maybe this was what he had in mind for a happy, easy life. My car was sitting in the LA airport, so I phoned my friend Josh there and told him I would send him the keys. He said he would take care of it, and I told him to use it until I decided if I was going to stay.

In a bar having a cold beer, this gorgeous women sat next to me with a little boy, and they both ordered a coke. We got to talking, and I told her about our Molokai adventure, and she smiled at me with interest in her face. When I found out she was divorced and lived in town, I knew I was not going back to New York.

We swam, we sailed, we made castles on the beach, and I was overboard. She had totally captured my heart. I thought maybe I should start looking for a job in one of the hotels, so I could survive as the money ran out, and be a solid citizen.

She was supposed to meet me for dinner at the Seagull, but never showed up. I phoned her number on the cell phone, but there was no answer. I was scared and worried, because tonight I was about to mention marriage. Did she sense it and chicken out?

When I met Ray, he said he was in the bar at the small indoor mall and saw Kay in there with a good-looking man who was holding her hand. He said, "I heard the waiter talk to him like he knew him. His last name was the same as Kay's, and she was quite taken with him, looking him in his eyes and smiling through the dinner."

I could only guess it was her ex-husband who had come back to talk her into a second chance. He was the one that was running around with other women on the beach, so I was shocked she would still be interested after the way she seemed to hate him in her conversation.

She phoned me early in the morning and told me they were giving it another try because they still loved one another, and he was the boy's father.

I was out of there on the next plane and phoned Josh to say I would now need the Ford. My clothes were in the trunk, as I slowly headed east, and at times could hardly see the road from the tears rolling across my eyes. They kept me company for three thousand miles, and I looked like a man with a terrible allergy. When George and Pete met me for a beer, they kept saying what a lucky son of a gun I was, and could not believe Ray liked it so much he would move there. They said we should all save our money and take a trip there together.

They wanted me to tell them all about it. Suddenly, tears flowed down my face like a child, and I could not talk and had to get out of there and leave. That was a few years back, and to this day I have never explained what hit me in the bar. The boys don't ask, and I have cried in many beers since. Every time an ad for a trip to the islands rolls across the television, old memories flood my mind. The boys met Ray on the island, since they finally made the trip, but I would not go with them. They had a wonderful time seeing Maui. Ray invited them for dinner before they were due to fly back to New York. He had a beautiful woman with him named Kay, and she asked for you. They were living in his nice condo, and it seems that they were married just two months ago.

Adonis

We were sitting in the office when the manager brought in the new vice president and introduced him to all the secretaries and bookkeepers. He looked like a movie actor and was drop dead handsome. Some of the women took a deep sigh, but I decided I would keep my cool, and just say, "How do you do, Mr. Stark." By the next day, the gals were bringing him coffee, a donut, and a flower on his desk. He seemed to expect all this special treatment and swooning, so I guess other jobs had produced the same treatment from the women employees.

He started working his way through the desks of females and asked the best looking dish out for a long lunch. He gave her special attentions with some evening dinners and "Come up to my apartment for a nightcap," if you know what I mean. Two weeks later, he would drop her and invite another good looking young thing out to lunch, then dinner, and a night cap, until he moved on to another pasture in two more weeks. I rather gathered that this routine had been played before, and it took him six weeks to finally get to my desk with a lunch invitation. I didn't jump at it like the others, but hesitated before accepting. Then it was time for the evening dinner and evening drink, and I played along for the experience. After the nightcap, he expected some entertainment in the bedroom, but I slowly picked up my purse and thanked him for the nice dinner and evening, and let myself out. Of course, being a smart gal, I got stuck for a very high taxi tab, and for what that cost, I could have taken him out to dinner.

Shoot, it's all part of the game, and I got a few free lunches out of it, to say nothing of one delicious, expensive dinner. Subtracting the taxi, I came out ahead by being independent, hard to get, and definitely not taken in by his beauty. This must have been the first challenge in a long time, because he was right back at my desk asking me out for lunch again. Well, I figured it was my turn at two weeks with the Adonis, so we went to the club for wine and lunch, and I accepted an invitation to a Broadway show.

Sitting in the fourth row center, I had to figure that he put some cash out for these center seats, so I was nice to him, but with great reserve, and did not gush over him like the other young things in the office. Of course after the show, with a snack at a bar with a drink, he invited me back to his place for the usual nightcap. I told him thanks, but it was late, and I had to get up early in the morning. He seemed slightly shocked, but did not want to give me the look of his disappointment.

Believe it or not, he was now challenged, since I think gals just did not turn him down for the late night drink and romp. By now, my two weeks trial was up, but he kept coming back for more meals, shows, and nightcaps. This made him more determined, but it also gave me more fortitude to not travel his usual route.

By now, the other girls in the office were mad at me,

because I was still afloat after one month. I think he was getting discouraged and running out of dinners and shows with me. Thus, I figured my run was over, and he would shift to some of the other good-looking girls. God knows, there were plenty of them sitting behind desks looking him over every time he passed through our computer chamber. Most of them were still falling over him with coffee, flowers, and giving him smiles that looked like a toothpaste ad.

When I looked up at four PM after doing some hard figures on the books, his face was above my desk inviting me to grab a bite and a movie. Of course I accepted, but let him know I was not into nightcaps later, and he could forget it and move down the chain of females, since a stampede of them were at his beck and call. No, he hung tight, and we left after work. After the movie, we had one drink in the bar, and I told him it was bedtime.

Now, one of the young innocent, not too experienced gals in the next office really had a crush on him like a teenager. She would ask me about our dates and started stalking him at his apartment, his dinners, shows, and such and seemed to know every move he made. She was giving me a hard time about him and was over the hill mentally on his adventures. I let her know right away that my dates were down to a few meals and movies, because she had a look in her eyes that said something upstairs was bananas. This type of women could be dangerous when she was so jealous and obsessed with one man. He did not seem to be interested in her, and had dropped her in one of his first dating rounds.

I had lunch with him one day and mentioned that he was being stalked by Phyllis in the other office. He was quite surprised and fluffed it off, but I told him he should really take heed. By then, I had backed off from some of his invitations, because there was something about him that ran a red flag in his conversations, for never did he sound too interested in any one woman, including me. He was not looking for a permanent arrangement.

Phyllis kept phoning me on her cell phone, and she saw him in the restaurant holding this woman's hand and kissing her passionately at the door outside. Never did he kiss Phyllis at all, and only slept with her after the evening drink. This woman was holding him tight like they were true loves, and Phyllis was hurrying to his apartment ahead of them. I told her not to do that, but she hung up on me.

The next day at the office, the police came to my desk asking all kinds of questions about Mr. Stark, and some on the woman that worked here, Phyllis Moore. I remembered that Phyllis did not come into work today, and I wondered what all the questioning encompassed. "Well, it seems Phyllis had somehow had a key made to his apartment and would hide in the closet in his bedroom so she could watch every encounter with women that took place. That included your nightcaps, but she said you were the only one that did not succumb to his bed. This woman that kept hanging on him and was kissing him was not from the office, and he made such a fuss over her that Phyllis could not contain her rage. She brought a gun to the closet, and when they were in a passionate act, she jumped out and began yelling at him for making love, and dropping her, and her jealous stalking nature got the better of her, and she shot the woman in the head at close range. Mr. Stark thought he was next, but she ran out of the place at that point." He called the police crying so hard they could hardly understand him, but they recorded his sobbing words enough to make out the story, that his wife had just arrived, and that this Phyllis girl from the office shot her in the head in a jealous rage. He had two kids staying with his mother until his wife was settled, and now they had no mother.

Phyllis was still at large and showed up at my place crazy as a loon and saying, "You took him away from me." I tried to tell her he was married, and she shot his wife. Apparently, she never heard the television news, or looked at a newspaper to know whom she shot. Then she started in on me for taking up weeks of his time, so he did not ask her out, and she held the gun at her waist. It was pointed right at me. Yes, she shot me right in the bible, which was under my covers because my arms were cold, and I had just put it down for a second. I made believe I was dead, and frankly, it took the wind out of me, and I could not get any oxygen for a second. She was still in the room, and when she was picking up her purse, I hit her a hard blow on the head with the lamp, and she went down like a ton of bricks. The gun fell out of her hands, and I called 911.

Poor Mr. Stark had confessed to the police that he just was lonely for his wife, and that is why he asked all the girls in the office out, but had to drop them when they started getting serious. His wife had left him, and she finally decided to give him a second chance and come back to him to try out their new life in New York. With all the women he could have picked with his looks, he could not stand living his life without his wife and hanged himself in the apartment bathroom. His sad note was for his mother.

Wow, were the girls in shock at the office. Stark was

dead, his wife was dead, Phyllis Moore was in jail, but totally nuts and would probably go to a mental hospital for many years.

Ha, Ha, I was still a virgin, and was saving myself for a man that was not handsome like Cary Grant or Clark Gable, just a nice, caring, loving man. He turned out to be the new vice president, who became the president, and gave me two wonderful kids, a big house, a swimming pool, a new Corvette, a ski cabin, a diamond necklace, and a trip to Europe for our anniversary. He sure looked handsome to me.

House For Sale

The house next door was empty for two years. I would get after the bank to send someone out to clean up the mess in weeds and trash. Mind you, I was not above cutting a bit of the front yard at times and picking up plastic coffee cups, but I was not about to take over the maintenance of the place.

One morning as I was backing out of the driveway, the real estate broker was taking the sign off the yard, so I opened the car window to ask if it had sold.

"Yes, and they are closing in the morning."

The van appeared a week later, and this gorgeous blond shook my hand to introduce herself and mentioned that her husband had been transferred to the office here. My God, she looked thirty-five and floored me when she said her 17-year-old son was at the Naval station in Norfolk. When my wife got a look at her, she was not quite as impressed with her beauty, and her location only a hundred yards from her door was not too thrilling either.

Since her husband was on a business trip to Toronto, he would not be back for another week. Finally he showed up, and we went through our handshake, and I welcomed him to the neighborhood.

Weekends they both worked in the yard doing flower beds and perking the place up, thus eliminating the look of neglect that fell on the place for so long. I am ashamed to say I found myself watching her out my bedroom window, and even lowered myself to admit that I used my little telescope to look at some parts up close. Why I was so attracted to her baffles me to this day, since my wife was no slouch in looks or shape. It must have been the male call of the wild, for it seemed more like a testosterone surge, or midlife crisis sneaking up on me, and was turning it into a stupid compulsion. I found myself shooting photos of her with my telephoto lens. Then I would look at them on my computer and put the memory chip back in my camera, so no record of them would appear on the screen.

Now I was dreaming of her and waking up to thoughts of her body at breakfast, and not paying too much attention to the kitchen conversation my wife directed toward me between sips of coffee.

I took my camera to work, so I could sneak peeks of that beautiful body, and announced I was taking some photos of the ducks near the marsh. Yes, I shot a few ducks and printed them up on the computer to cover my backside.

The weather was turning cooler as the months moved into fall. This depressed me because there would not be too much reason to work in the yard any more. Also, it would be dark when I came home from work. I started printing up some photos and sticking them away so my wife would not view them. In my sneaky moments, I would pull them out and take them to work. Since Eleanor drove her own car and never used my business vehicle, I hid them in the car's instruction book.

As winter approached, I tried to talk Eleanor into

inviting our new neighbors over for dinner, but she said we can't, because we have so many of our old friends that we need to have here first. Well, that was true, and I tried to get her to include them with the old gang, but she was not inclined to get involved with new people, since we had nothing in common with people from New Jersey. I thought that was a strange reply because Fred and Sally were as removed in interest as the Queen of England is from a sea captain, but still, we entertained them.

The winter dragged on, and I tried looking in her bedroom window at times, but with the thin curtains it was like trying to focus your eyes through milk. Soon the spring would be here, and the yard work with it, so that meant exposure.

Now I would go out of my way to talk to her as she dug in the dirt and offered my help in the flowerbed. She always declined since her husband liked to do that when he came back from his business trip, but thanks anyhow. My wife did all of our flower beds and yard trimming. I just ran the lawn mower over the grass when it started looking high, and that was only when it really needed it.

My wife dropped me off at the airport, and I was only going to be gone four days. I did take my camera, in case I had to snap a few photos of our new building, but of course, I had the memory chip to view in the motel room.

When I got home, there was not much conversation, and life had changed in the kitchen over coffee. Only a few questions, like, how is the new building looking, and when will it be finished? Also, Eleanor had a headache more than usual at night and went to bed early.

When our neighbors were working in the front yard, I tried to be friendly, and he walked up to me and hit me smack on the nose with a hard punch. He then was winding up for a second blow, when I backed up and hurried home. As I was leaving, he started yelling at his wife and accusing her of having an affair with me. The last thing I heard as I held my handkerchief up to my bloody nose walking home was, "I want a divorce. No woman cheats on me."

My wife saw it all happen and said she would live with me, but not as man and wife.

It was all over my head, until I learned that the neighbor wanted to borrow the large screwdriver I kept in my glove compartment. He had to move the instruction book to get to it, and when he picked it up, out came the photos of his wife.

If no one is in the forest when a tree falls, does it make noise? If a man never touches a neighbor's wife, does a few photographs constitute infidelity?

That was five years ago, my neighbors moved because of me, and my wife still has a perpetual headache. The memory chip from my camera is buried behind the garage, and I don't take photos of ducks anymore. Now the house next door is empty again, and I am trimming a bit and picking up the yard trash. It feels like old times.

The Clinic

The girls at lunch would talk about the jerks they were dating, and how they all longed to meet someone that was more interested in them personally, marriage, and children. It seems most of their dates wanted to sit in a bar, watch a game, down beer, and finish the night with some quick sex. It was getting old. Maybe they were living in the wrong neighborhood or environment, and where were the real nice men, the old fashioned gentlemen, instead of these slobs. Well, I was embarrassed to agree with them, but I pretty well tried to meet nicer men at my hobby clubs, astronomy, and photography. Still, the pickings were slim.

My brother in Seattle loved animals, as I did, so he would send me photos of his three dogs, Red, White, and Blue, quite often, and we cut out photos in magazines and newspapers to swap. George had a flag on his wall in the kitchen, and two of his dogs would stand on their hind legs when he asked for a salute. Red and Blue would jump right up and do his command, but Old White just could not master the exercise and would sit and watch them.

George sent me a very cute photo of a pup that was in the animal shelter ad in the Seattle paper. I was about to cut it out, when I happened to flip over the page and caught the want ad column. A new veterinary hospital was about to open and needed help with someone with experience with cats and dogs at a vet clinic. Since I spent most of my spare time in college with such a part time job for four years, I felt I would qualify. The thought of starting a whole new job out of this one horse town excited me, so I phoned them right up to give them my background.

They seemed interested, since most of the applicants had little first hand experience with the actual vet procedure with domestic animals.

Because my brother lived nearby, he invited me for a visit so I could meet the vets first hand and see what they expected. They told me to report in on Monday because they were getting swamped with work from the shelter, because they gave their animals their first shots and neutered the male dogs and cats for a fee from the city.

Well, once I got into the swing of their operation, they hired me on the spot, since the routine was just like my vet work near college. My brother gave me the spare bedroom, and we really enjoyed one another's company. His dogs were so much fun that I loved getting up in the morning for the flag salute and a few free moments to romp with them. At night we went out for a walk, and I had Old White on a leash, and brother Dan took Red, and Blue. It was a nice neighborhood, and we would even go out in the dark without a worry, especially with our three guard dogs.

Two of the vets were married to one another, and the wife was smarter than her husband and seemed to figure out a mysterious illness that baffled the other doctors. She went out of her way to help me at times and always was kind to me in little things she did during our work hours. We also had some more free time once in a while and could slip out to a restaurant for a nice lunch and visit.

One of the gals that just helped wrap sores and cuts and fed the animals seemed to have a thing for my friend's husband. This could prove embarrassing at times, because he was encouraging her. It was obvious to all who worked there, so you know the wife had to recognize the sparks between them. They did not seem to try and hide their obvious attraction for one another.

At lunch, finally, my friend confessed that this affair was starting to get out of hand, since he was going out at night with some excuse or work related project. She followed him a couple of times, and of course he went right over to this gal's apartment. She was asking me for advice on how she should handle the situation, and of course I did not have a clue.

It kept getting worse, and she was humiliated in front of the other doctors, and workers and tried to keep a stiff upper lip in their presence. One of the nice vets, Peter, went out of his way to spend time with her and cater to her needs when he was free. He would bring her a sandwich when she could not leave during busy hours and generally be of some help. Of course, he knew what was going on in her marriage and rather liked her beyond just a working friendship. They started ignoring her husband to a degree, and he would join us in the little corner deli for lunch at times.

Now she told me that her husband was flaunting his romance, just totally doing his own thing, and going his own way. It struck her that she could live without him and the humiliation of his infidelity. She looked him in the eye and told him she had talked to her lawyer for a divorce and financial settlement. He looked surprised, and she mentioned that she had him followed, and his car went right to Flo's house night after night. He asked for forgiveness and said he would end it right away, "but don't leave me and break up our business." The reply left him speechless, as she informed him that it was too late and she wanted out and was moving on. Her lawyer got her a good financial settlement, and the husband had to pay her off and buy her half of the business in the agreement.

With the divorce, Peter felt free to take her out and wine and dine her, and he gave his notice and quit the ex-husband's establishment. They told me their plan for a small vet clinic, and would I come in with them for the help I could offer. It was a pleasure to drop out of the uncomfortable set up, because frankly her new boyfriend was decent and honest. Her ex-husband talked to the workers like they were slaves and morons. Most of the gang only worked for the clinic because she was so nice, and there was an undercurrent of unrest and hate for the unfaithful ass of a husband.

When we found an appropriate layout for the clinic, the set up was perfect. We got the city's contract for the animal shelter because the person in charge had some bad fights about the payment arrangement because they only paid every four months. That was the deal when the husband signed the contract, but he continued to give the finance office a hard time about it. So he lost that good money deal, and one by one the other vets started leaving him to work for the ex-wife. Then his girlfriend quit the job because she had a health issue and disappeared. She never even said goodbye, or why she was leaving. He pretty well lost his work operation, social life, and hot girlfriend.

His ex let him see their new clinic and showed him around to rub it in that they were all doing fine without him. Then when Peter sidled up to him to say hello, he also announced that they were running the clinic as man and wife and were most happy. Oh, and by the way, your girlfriend Flo talked to me about her problem, and I sent her to my doctor friend at the hospital in San Francisco. It seems her health was going down the tubes faster than she expected. That HIV infection is very difficult to control and she was losing ground week by week, but I'm sure she told you all about it.

The Golden Years

It was just an old boarding house, with four bedrooms upstairs, and one bathroom. Everyone had a chamber pot under the bed to save their bladders when someone would hog the john for a shower or bath. It was not the house where the owner prepared meals in grand style on their long table with happy eaters. We had two burners built into a unit that had a sink a foot long and a foot wide. The fridge was underneath the sink and burners. I washed my face and hair over that square sink so many times my back automatically bent over when I got near it.

I had been looking for my own low rent apartment, but anything that sounded good was in a location with crime, noise, drug dealers, and low life. When you only depended on your social security, it was low rent or nothing. The bedroom living was better than no shelter and was in a decent neighborhood, but was very confining, since the living room was off limits to borders. Our televisions were the only company any of us had there.

The paper kept showing a new place going up for the elderly, and it was out of the city limits where they had lots of property. Thus, they were able to build it on ground level. There were no stairs or elevators, and you had to be over sixty-five to live there. My name had been on the list for a year while it was going up. Finally, the mayor cut the ribbon, and a letter came in the mail, so I started packing my few things for the move. A van marked "Peaceful Acres" picked me up with my bags, and the ride in the country in itself was a joy, for those four walls were not too inspirational.

My name was on A 16, but first they gave us a slight tour, since they provided a small pharmacy and grocery store for our needs. The food prices were cheaper than the regular store, and it was quite a walk with my little portable basket for food in the boarding house location. This one was close and on the same property. If you were sick, they would deliver. Well, needless to say, someone prepared this layout with us old folks in mind. My small apartment was perfect, for I had my own shower, sink and john, a small kitchen, with a real size sink, and gas stove and fridge. It was such a pleasure to use the shower without someone pounding on the door to get into the bathroom that I sang with my happiness.

My neighbor was elderly compared to my 72 years, and she invited me in for a cup of tea. You could tell she had come from a smart background, but she did not flaunt it. We became good friends instantly and, like me, she got by on her social security. She had some bad arthritis, so I helped her at times, and would wash her breakfast dishes after our tea time and take out her old papers and magazines, so she would not have to deal with it. Her late husband had his own business, but hit hard times. He died without insurance, because he did not believe in it. There was not too much money in the kitty after the business failed, in fact, debt followed him for years. Thank God for social security and this wonderful place for her remaining days.

It was easy living when the weather got bad because they had a little bus that would take us to our doctor appointments and to the grocery store if we wanted to look around the aisles and see the actual food instead of phoning for deliveries. We got a bit of exercise by starting at one end of the store and walking up and down each aisle with our carriage. When it rained, I enjoyed that walk.

My neighbor was taken sick and just felt terrible for days, but would not go to the doctor at her age, so I just made her some chicken soup and toast, so she would not starve. She hung on for a long time and always showed me where she kept her papers. It seems she had a no-account son, who only visited her and the husband when he wanted money. Was he concerned about his old parents, not at all, but his trip always ended up for a request for cash, like he deserved it. He never seemed to have a job, but needed money for a new deal that was going to make him all kinds of wealth. He was ugly on his last visit when he found out they had no money to give. They were on their social security only, and he wanted some of that. He was informed that it was already eaten up for rent, food, and blood pressure pills. He thought he would come back next month to pick up some of the cash, but was informed that the check went directly into the bank, and the bank paid the bills for them, so cash was nonexistent. That was the last time they saw him. He did not know his father had died, and probably would not have cared upon hearing the news. They adopted him when his mother died of TB, and he was always trouble.

She seemed to go downhill and ate less and less. Her words to me when I would leave after feeding her was, "Don't forget to take my papers and the suitcase under the bed. I don't want my son ever to have anything that is in it. My rings are in there, and the engagement one is a nice diamond, and I want you to have it. You must not forget to take it, for I never want him to get his hands on my personal items."

I heard this story every time I did something for her. She lost even her appetite for my little tasty snacks with tea, so I would give her chicken broth to keep her alive. Her blood pressure was so low, she did not need her pills.

When I came in to see her at bedtime, I tried to get some food in her and suggested a doctor, but she said, at 89, she did not want to think of hospitals. Would I just give her some cold water and talk to her.

Thus, I told her about my husband and his little shop, and how I did the books for years, until he could afford to get a bookkeeper so I could enjoy our home. She grabbed my hand and told me to take her papers and the suitcase tonight, for she had a feeling her son was coming to pester her for money. She just did not have the strength to deal with him. I tried to make her rest easy and not worry about him, but she would not let me out of the place without the case and papers. When I lifted it, it was very heavy for my old bones, but I pushed it out on the bottom wheels. She seemed relieved, and I told her I would be back at breakfast time.

In the morning I put her spare key in the door so not to wake her, but her face was in a peaceful smile, and she looked white. I was afraid death had taken her soul during the night.

The home provided for her remains to be cremated, and no one knew where to locate her son, since he had some deal in South America, according to his last words to her, and never a card to let her know his new location.

With great effort, I got the suitcase on my end table. I had to play with the key she gave me and finally managed to open the rusty lock. The top layer was all newspaper clippings of her days as an opera singer, and I was shocked to see where she had performed, Italy, London, Australia, and New York. She gave up traveling when she met her husband, and their wedding picture was in one of the papers, and they were both handsome. As I got under the papers, there was a velvet bag contained the biggest diamond engagement ring a women could hold on one finger. It was worth a fortune. I lifted the next papers on her husband's business during the war, and how essential it was to the war effort, and I read everything from top to bottom. I was sad that she had not told me about her career life, for I would have loved the stories of the opera days and the many trips.

When I lifted the papers completely out of the thick bag, I fell back in shock. My eyes fell upon stack after stack of hundred dollar bills. No wonder the case was so heavy. My goodness, there had to be thousands of dollars in cash in the pile. It looked like too many to count, and I was beyond attempting it for weeks. When I took out her papers, like she requested, there was a letter to me in her shaky handwriting. "Everything in this bag is for you and your future. It is honest money I made in my career and saved for an emergency, and my son will never see it because he was a selfish kid from the first day he could talk. You are my best friend and have done deeds that were beyond friendship. Buy yourself a new television and take that trip to New Zealand that you would mention to me so often. I'll be right there with you, and under the money you will find one of my recordings on a cassette, so you can hear what voice your old friend had on the many stages of the world. I love you as a sister and bless you for all the kind acts that were bestowed on this old neighbor. God Bless you, Blanche Wright."

I cried for her because I truly missed her company and our tea talks. When I heard her voice on the tape, tears flowed down my cheeks, because it was beautiful, and when I saw her stage name, I remembered it in my music appreciation class in high school. She was my friend, and I never knew who she really was, only Blanche. My music teacher would have been floored if she knew who was my neighbor, and certainly my husband, for he sprang for one of her concerts when we were first married, and it was one of the big thrills of my life.

When I paid for my New Zealand trip with cash, the girl raised her eyebrows. I laughed and said it just seemed to build up in a suitcase under my bed, so don't underestimate the power of saving a dollar.

No one ever heard from her son at the rest home, and I guess he figured his parents were not a soft touch, so why should he bother with them. Had he been just a little considerate of his Mother, he now would be taking this trip instead of me, which goes to show you that being ungrateful, selfish, and unkind has its own reward, a kick in the pants.

Traveler

My husband only had a month of tour duty left before coming home to me. I spent a lot of time sitting on the back deck writing letters to him. When the phone rang, I went in to answer it and talked for a short time with my neighbor, Mary Scott, or Mary Queen of Scotts as we teased her.

When I came back outside, there was a large, strange dog sitting on my patio trying to drink the water from a slow drip in my faucet. His front paws were full of dirt, so I knew he dug under my privacy fence. He had very long legs, and his body was so lean I knew he was starving. He backed away from me, and I filled my green pail full to the brim with water and stood back. He ran to it, and drank like he just spent a week on the Sahara Desert. I know you can live without food for a long time, but three or four days without fluid and you are either dead or close to it.

He finally got his fill and slumped on the cement in the shade, but not close to my chair. Well, I could not stand to see him that lean and went in the kitchen and filled a bowl with my meat loaf, after chopping it up in small pieces. When my old dog, Flag, was alive, I had a big bag of dog food and treats, but he was now gone six months, and everything was tossed, except maybe some rawhide chewys. When he got a whiff of the food, he stood right up and held off until I put it down and backed away from his comfort zone. Watching him eat, I was thinking he may have some wolf in him, for it seemed to go down in one whole gulp. Certainly, there was no point in breaking it up in bits.

He now seemed content and had a nice face, though gaunt, because of his lean appearance. Still, he held his distance, and I had no fear of his presence because he just seemed thirsty and hungry. Now his eyes slowly closed, and he fell asleep. He looked like he had been traveling and just needed some comfort. I could see where he came in under the back fence, because you could see light through the hole. There was a big field back there, and some arroyos where the rainwater flowed down the side hills.

When I finished my letter, he was still sleeping, and it was late in the afternoon, so it would be dark soon. I carried a pot of water to the shed and put down some old carpet I had in there and made him a bed. There was a Dutch door on it, so I could then leave the top closed, and tie the bottom one back so the wind would not catch it. I found one of Flag's rawhide chewys and put it on the carpet, for it could get cold at night at this altitude. I just called him, made some clicking noises, picked up the rawhide and showed it to him, and threw it back inside the door. Then I gave him his safety space again and went in the back door. Through the window, I could see him slide in the door and flop on the carpet. The chewy was in his mouth, and he would probably be occupied for a long time gnawing at it.

In the morning he was still there, for I could see his head on the carpet near the door. I had a large tin of salmon and put that in the bowl near the kitchen door, and added water to top off the pail. Then I stepped inside the door with my eyes at the window. He came right up, did his big gulp, and the fish disappeared.

Well, this went on for a week, and on the weekend I was sitting in my chair writing to Tom telling him about the big dog, when suddenly he got up and walked to the back fence, and out the hole. This gave me a bit of a scare, because he was a comfort to me being just around, since I would talk to him all the time, and he seemed to like that and would cock his head to the side when I spoke. When I stood on my little block of wood, I could see over the fence, and he was just in the field doing his morning duty and came right back through the opening to the shaded deck. I told him he was a gentleman not to soil the yard.

He seemed to now be my dog, for I had bought a large bag of dog food and treats, but worried how I was going to get him to the vet because he could be needing shots. I did not want to rush it and scare him off, so I talked to the vet, and he said, "Give him a few days, and on my way home, I'll stop by and see him."

When I put the pad down, I just closed my eyes for a minute, and my arm was hanging by the side of the chair. Suddenly I felt a wet tongue on the back of my hand, and he had licked me a thanks and moved next to me so I could finally pet him. That was it, so I had to come up with a name, and settled on General Lee's name for his horse, Traveler. Of course his nickname turned out to be Trave, and in a short time he would respond to it, especially when I called him for dinner. Thus Tom and I had a dog.

The vet gave him shots and petted him, and he was gentle and trusting while I was nearby. Now that he was getting two squares a day, his body was filling out, and he looked like a bear he was that big.

My day arrived, and I went to the airport to pick up Tom, and we threw our arms around each other in pure joy. He was so happy to come home, and when he saw Traveler, he could not believe how big he was and carefully called him by name. Trave went right up to him after I told him it was all right, and once he figured he was living in the house, decided he must be family. By then, he was sleeping in our bedroom, and Tom would romp and play with him so they became close pals in no time.

Now when Tom had to go to the hardware store for a few things, Trave sat right next to him in the front seat, and they both went shopping. Apparently while turning the corner a few miles from our house, the engine cut off, and when it did, the power steering went off with it, and Tom lost the feel of the wheel and hit the tree hard. Trave fell to the floor and was all right, but Tom seemed to be unconscious. There was smoke coming out of the engine, and a fire flared up in a short time. Trave was trying to pull Tom outside, because the doors had popped open. He could not manage him because of the seat belt, and like all dogs, the only tool he had was a good set of teeth, so he put them to work and chewed the belt off in a short time. He got Tom by the collar of his light leather jacket and just pulled until his legs dropped on the pavement. Slowly, he could drag him inch by inch away from the car.

It was a back country road, so no other cars had passed

this stretch of roadway as yet. The flames were getting larger as Trave moved him toward the grass. The gas tank exploded like a bomb, and the car was consumed in flames. By then, Tom was on the edge of the weeds on the other side of the road. Finely a car arrived, and when the man approached Tom, Trave pulled him another foot and then ran away. The cell phone brought the ambulance in no time, and the hospital phoned me, so I had to get a taxi.

The man told the ambulance driver and crew how the dog had pulled the man across the road and licked his face before he left him.

When I got to Tom's room, he was awake with a very bad concussion. He talked softly to me and said he did not remember anything except Trave kissed him goodbye and told him he would be all right. I smiled at that.

The hospital would keep him for a week or ten days until he felt better.

I worried about Traveler when I heard he ran away. My heart was in my throat as the taxi took me home and when I came out the kitchen door, there he was on the deck. He ran to me, and I put my arms around him, and I hugged him tight while thanking him for saving Tom's life.

He licked my tears as a few ran down my cheek, and I heard, "Tom will be all right."

I thought, am I hearing things? I looked at Traveler and said, "Did you just talk to me, or am I dreaming?"

His lips curled back against his mouth in a big smile, and he winked at me, honest. I swear it was a wink.

Nine Months

There was going to be a baby in less than nine months. The father had money, a big house, and a great business. The mother was a farm girl from Iowa, but smart, well read, and had social graces. He was her first love, but always he had a mistrust of women in general. He thought she was superior to most that he had dated, and certainly she had looks that none of the other sophisticated gals could touch. Yet that suspicion was an undercurrent in his makeup he never could quite shake.

When she said she was pregnant, he just knew it was not his baby. He told her as much and she was devastated, for he was the only man she ever loved, and who ever made love to her. He let her know that he would not accept it as his offspring, and that if she wanted to continue seeing him, an abortion would have to take place very soon. She was shocked at his coldness and his accusations of her being a loose woman. She let him know that she would keep the baby and not bother him for money, or any financial help in raising the child. Her ultrasound showed a little boy, and she was thrilled more than she had expected. She might have to go back to Iowa to have the delivery, but her parents were loving and understanding, so she did not worry about being excommunicated by her mother or father. If he wanted to think the worst of her, and not take any responsibility for the pregnancy, that was fine, because she would raise the boy and give him a good life without this selfish ex-lover.

She met him for lunch, cleansed him of any responsibility, and told him of her plans for Iowa and the farm. He never blinked once or offered her one dollar. She told him that he was the only man she ever loved and was sorry he did not love her enough to trust her and want to share in the baby's life. They parted with a cold handshake, and she told him she would send him a photo of his child after the birth.

Once she was with her family, they came to her aid with love and money, and never condemned her for her situation. However, they were glad she came home, and parted from the big evil city. As she grew larger, her maternal love poured out for her unborn boy, and she knew it would grow deeper with each month she carried it.

With the whole family at the hospital, including her sisters, their husbands, and brothers and parents, she produced this perfect new life. He was whole in toe count and health. Gifts were supplied by everyone, and he lacked for nothing in the usual needs for a nursery.

As he got a little older and lost the new born face of wrinkles, he showed good looks. She sent the photo to the father in New York. He studied it, put it on the mantel, and would say, he is cute, but definitely not mine.

While walking him in the carriage on one Sunday morning, she met her old college boyfriend, who was now a lawyer in town. He picked the baby up, and just played with it, and talked to him about his mother in school, and how he missed her when she took a job in the big city. Then he glanced at her with a request to go to dinner, and to bring the baby. They could manage him all right at the drive-in, since he could sleep on the back seat, and this would give them a chance to catch up on their lives since they last saw one another. He had served in the army as a captain and had a few serious affairs, but nothing earth shattering, and certainly none of them moved him like she did. She was quite touched by what he said, and pretty soon they were into serious talk about marriage. He still loved her, and the baby was wonderful, and he never asked her about the father, or how she met him, or anything that took place in her New York life.

When they were married, he was the best father a woman could desire, and the baby would light up every time he came home from the office. He did not have the money of the man in the city, but their home was fine, and he helped her change diapers, and he loved to be with her every free minute he could get away from business.

The father in New York had his mother for lunch at his plush apartment, and as she walked by the mantel over the fireplace, there stood the baby's photo. She stopped cold and asked him about it. He confessed that his old girlfriend sent it to him, but it was not his baby. The mother asked if he was sure, and he said absolutely. At that she opened her purse and reached for her wallet, and out came a photo of a little boy around the same age. She handed it to him, and he looked at it in disbelief, for they were identical. His mother said these two boys came from the same mold, and I think you are wrong about your judgment on fatherhood.

When he phoned her number in Iowa, his thoughts ran to marriage, fixing a nursery room, and settling down with the one woman whom he truly missed. She was honest, lovely, never pressured him for money at any time, and seemed to be determined to raise the boy herself. This woman had pluck, and he suddenly admired her, especially after seeing both photographs. When the girl's mother answered the call, she gave him her phone number, and he dialed it with anticipation. A man answered after a couple of rings, and he hesitated in asking for her by name, but finally said, "Is Robyn there?"

The male voice replied, "My wife is out shopping, let me have your name, and I'll tell her you called."

Oregon Bound

Jeff and I were both trying to figure out how to manage a trip to Oregon to visit my older brother. Once we were there, we could stay at his place and see that part of the country with a roof over our heads. We cut lawns and did odd jobs, and had enough for spending money, but we were unable to save enough for air fare. It occurred to me that at eighteen, we could hitchhike to the coast and have enough pin money to get by with our needs. The weather was warm, and we had some light sleeping bags, so could spread our gear under a tree, camp, and cook some beans and franks from a can, and get by.

Our parents were not too thrilled with the idea, but since there were two of us, they could see the safety in numbers. We were young males and healthy, and could take care of ourselves. We went to my room to make a list of the clothes, cooking gear, a two-man nylon tent, and food items. I stuffed my camera in my backpack and kissed my folks goodbye. We told them we would call them from time to time on Jeff's cell phone.

Jeff's dad drove us to the highway on his way to work, and out went our thumbs for the Northwest. It was rather exciting, since we had never been too far from home, or any place miles beyond the state borders. We walked for about an hour, kept putting our thumbs out, and were smart enough to carry water. Our thirst in the sun picked up with the higher temperatures, and pretty soon my bottle was empty. This gave me some stress and insecurity, but about that time a big truck stopped and asked us where we were headed. When we said Oregon, he laughed because he was only going to the next town, but thought we might have a better chance for a ride at the truck stop there.

We thanked him, and I saved my empty bottle and filled it with fresh water from the tap in the men's room so I did not have to buy one. We were able to get a burger there for a few bucks each and were content that we had moved away from our hometown. We could not pick up a truck heading West and did not land our next ride until late in the afternoon, when an older women and her son picked us up. We had to get out when she was turning south off the highway. We spotted a good spot to camp and jumped the fence to get under a big tree for the night. It was far enough off the road so no one would bother us. I had a little alcohol stove in my pack, so we heated up a dry package of chicken soup, and we gobbled some bread to satisfy our hunger. We set up the tent, as dark clouds started moving in our direction. We crawled inside after we put our packs in plastic garbage bags to keep them dry. I was sorry we did not move away from the tree when we heard the thunder and saw the flashes of lightning. The rain bounced off our tent for twenty minutes, and we felt snug in our nylon enclosure. In spite of the threat, we fell asleep, and never did get hit by a bolt.

On the road again, a fellow in his fifties picked us up and gave us a long ride for most of the day. He offered to put us up for the night as we neared his home. Since the sky was still overcast with rain clouds and looked stormy, we accepted with thanks. He bought a very large pizza to fill the three of us and took us to his farmhouse. We were stuffed and tired, and he offered us his son's den in the basement. It had a couple of cots and a single john and sink, which was perfect. Wow, what a storm we had that night, and we were saying how lucky we were to find this nice dry set up. In the early morning, I thought I heard a car pull away from the house. We were hungry, so quickly got dressed with our packs, and thought we would head out for the day. When Jeff put his hand on the doorknob, it was locked. Also it was made of steel, which we never noticed when we first arrived last night. We started yelling and pounding against the door, but realized we were trapped. We thought of the cell phone, but it just would not pick up a signal from this sealed tomb.

We started investigating the physical layout of the den and noticed there were no windows. The little room off it had some canned goods, so we helped ourselves to some cold tins for breakfast. There was a huge old safe in there, so we started to wonder what we fell into. Also there were photos of young boys our age all over the walls, thus Jeff deduced from their ages that this guy was some predator, and we were the prey.

In our gear we had knives and camping items to use on the door and safe. I tried to work the lock under the knob, but it had a cross bar on the back of it. Jeff was interested in the old tumblers on the heavy safe. He was very smart with high tech computers and electronics, and was having fun spinning the numbered dial and putting his ear to the metal near it. He played with it most of the day, About six o'clock, we heard a car pull alongside the house, and a short time afterwards the door opened as he came down a few steps with a gun and told us to back up while he left two chicken dinners. He told us to put our money and personal items on the mid step, including our watches. Jeff had an expensive one ,a graduation gift, and mine was an old Timex. Then the door slammed closed with a metal thud. Of course, we ate the meal with fear in our backbone, and started yelling to him to let us out, but he never answered.

Another night went by, and Jeff played with the safe while I looked around for some escape route. We decided it was just a matter of time until he got down to his business with us, so we better make a plan right now. There was a low shelf near the door, and we moved all the paint cans and junk from it, which left enough room for me to hide there if I folded my legs. We had found some hockey sticks, gloves and a baseball bat, so Jeff told me to wait until he walked down a few stairs with the gun and to get behind him. Then give him a strong whack with the bat, but don't do it if it looks like he is going to shoot. We waited all day knowing he would return for dinner.

I got on the cot scared stiff and wished we had cut more lawns and taken a plane west instead of hitting the road in our hiking boots. In time, I must have fallen asleep and left Jeff still working on the safe while I drifted into a deep dream. Later, he must have been sick during the night because I heard the toilet flush many times in my half foggy state. By the wall clock it was seven in the morning, and we could hear the car pull out the driveway. We did not hear him return until six-thirty PM. By then I was in the shelf with the bat, and our predator opened the door with a bag of burgers in his left hand. He had the gun pointed at Jeff on the cot, who said he was feeling sick. The man took a few steps, looked around the room, and asked where I was, and whack, I hit him so hard he fell down the rest of the flight of stairs, and Jeff was on him. We beat him up like two thugs, and I think I broke a few bones in his leg and arm with the bat. We grabbed the gun, took our packs, and ran to the kitchen. Jeff shook the bullets out of the gun and stuck it in the fridge.

The car keys were on a hook by the door, so Jeff handed them to me to drive. You could hear both of us breathing like we ran the Boston Marathon. Into the car we jumped, and it flew down the dirt road to the mailbox. We left it parked there and hurried up the road trying to get our wind and move away from the place. Finally, we got a ride to town in the back of a pickup truck. Jeff made a note of the name on the mailbox and the road marker, so we would remember the location of the place. My hand went to my boot, and I pulled out my ten dollars emergency money. We borrowed a piece of paper and a pen in the café and sat at the table while we drank coffee. Jeff wrote the whole story for the police so they could drive out and nail the SOB. I never read it, but it seemed like a long letter. We did not want to tell them in person because they would hold us in town to testify.

We did not spend enough time in his house looking for our possessions, because we rushed out of there like two crazy kids.

I was complaining to him about having no money for a decent meal, and maybe we should phone home and get our parents to send us a money order, so we could continue our trip. He told me not to worry and hailed a cab with his arm. He directed the driver to take us to the airport. I was sputtering since I knew we were broke. When we arrived he paid the man with a hundred dollar bill. He then dragged me to the counter for two standby tickets to Portland. I followed him like a puppy dog to the best restaurant in the place asking him a million questions. He ordered two large steak dinners, and he could not answer me because we were too hungry to talk. He opened his pack and showed me a mother load of hundred dollar bills in stacks. My mouth fell open while he lifted his right hand and spread his fingertips. Some of them were still bleeding a bit .He had filed them with his Swiss army knife.

"These little devils cracked the combination of that bloody old safe. There were drugs inside it, and I flushed most of them down the toilet last night so he could not sell them if he tried to get out of there before the police arrived, if we were lucky enough to escape from him. I left enough on the shelf for the law to find so they could arrest him on a drug charge. Since he interrupted our trip, which was a great inconvenience, I decided he should compensate us. Oh, I forgot one thing," as he rattled the car keys, and dropped them in the mailbox. "Our friend won't need these for a few years."

He gave me the time off his watch and handed me my gold chain and coin. He smiled and announced our host had kept them in the glove compartment, and I never even saw him open it, I was that intent on driving to the highway. He handed me a Rolex and dangled another one off his finger and said, "This one is a gift for your brother. I did not have enough time to look at the rest of the items."

When we phoned home, we told our families we were lucky to catch a ride straight through to Portland and apologized for not phoning sooner, and of course we caught hell for worrying them.

My brother was impressed when he put the watch on his wrist. We told him we got lucky at one of the casinos where we stopped for lunch. We all went out for a prime rib dinner and ate with gusto.

That was our adventure when we were eighteen. Jeff is now the head of a very large computer outfit, and has made loads of money on his patents. I have a small sports store. Our casino money gave both of us a good start in life and business. Now, we do reminisce over a few beers on occasion, however, never in front of our kids.

Back In The Thirties

In the nineteen thirties, I was a young girl living with my grandparents in a tiny bungalow in a small Texas town. The little house only had one bedroom and my grandparents slept there. I had a studio couch in the back hall near the front closet they used for a storage room. My hall bedroom had a pipe across the length of the hall opposite my couch. It was so high I had to stand on a chair to hang my coat, school dresses, and sweaters on it. This left room underneath for a small dresser where I kept my personal items like my hairbrush and comb, plus my socks and undergarments.

The house had no dining room, just a small kitchen with the usual sink, apartment size stove, and a small fridge. We were lucky because some of the neighbors were still using the small iceboxes of that time. That was the only source for keeping food cool so it would not spoil on those hot summer days. The iceman was a friendly sight on our back dirt road, and he knew us all by name.

When we would sit down to eat a meal together, it was on a square card table in the corner of the living room near the kitchen door.

My birth mother had disappeared with her lazy boyfriend one night when I was a year old, so I never knew her or my real father. My grandparents never mentioned her name, and I suspected she was a big disappointment in their life. Frankly, I guessed she had never married and probably was not sure who truly was my biological father.

I was so young when my mother left me that I never longed for her, and had accepted my grandparents as my mother and father, and I called them Mom and Dad. My grandmother was the only maternal thread I had ever known, so it was interesting how one adjusted to the life that was dealt to us, and I accepted mine without complaint or question.

My grandfather had a small railroad pension, so we watched our nickels and dimes like they were pieces of gold. Every penny went into a calculated budget. We baked many dishes, bought eggs by the half dozen, and never had the luxury of more than one egg on our plate at a time. My grandmother baked her own bread to save money, and a thin spread of butter with some homemade jam would be a good sandwich for lunch. Peanut butter was only bought once in a blue moon, and we would put it on saltines for a snack in the late afternoon. Coffee was too expensive so we lived on the cheapest Atlantic and Pacific store brand tea we could find.

My Uncle Fred lost his job and had always been busy with work as a fine carpenter. He had no place to live, and was my grandmother's brother. Thus, he came to live with us and brought all his tools and some left over lumber with him. You can't believe how he improved the house and the little storage room, since he went right to work building shelves in there from the floor to the ceiling. He moved all our tins of stored rice, flour, beans, and sugar off the floor, and even had room above for his shirts and pants and socks. He built a small cot that just reached from one end of the closet to the other, and had it been one foot shorter he could not have stretched his full length out to sleep. The saving grace was a small window, since that wall was in the front of the house, and they had put one in there for air when it was built. It gave him light during the day, unlike my hall room.

Fred built a rack hanger in the kitchen, and the house was so old all the ceilings were very high. On the rack he hung the bags of carrots, potatoes, and onions that had been stored in his small room. He had a rope attached to the frame by a hook, and it was raised out of our reach so we could just lower it when we needed some vegetables to cook.

Uncle Fred was a gem because he could build or fix anything and took the good and the bad in his stride with a smile. He got me taking out the good classics at the local library, and the both of us would spend a lot of evenings there until closing time. We could not afford the movies, so his choice of books for me were wonderful, and I would get totally lost in exciting stories until bedtime, and the adventures of Tom Sawyer and Huck Finn would linger with me until sleep captured my thoughts and I drifted into the unconscious dreams of childhood.

My girlfriend, Sadie, had a radio, and every day at lunch in school she would tell me about the different stories that were scary, exciting, and funny. I just could not imagine getting all that wonderful entertainment in your own living room. Mind you, I was not complaining because I was so thrilled to have the library books and the stories from Sadie, that my life was truly full. Besides, we would not have any money for such a luxury as a radio in this Depression, so I would not ever wonder about such an extravagance. Sadie was always anxious to share the stories with me, so I felt quite privileged to have such a good friend.

Uncle Fred told me to take only one book at a time from the library to read because I would have time to finish it then. If you were late in returning it, the late fee that the library would impose on it after two weeks was a two-cent charge for every day you were late. Because I was always on time, I would always be free of debt. Since I had absolutely no money of my own, I was very careful on this point. Once Uncle Fred took my book back for me when I caught the flu, and he informed me that when I was well, the book could again be borrowed, so I could know how it ended.

Christmas was coming, so we were making little gifts for our parents in school. I was sewing a handkerchief for my mother and a scarf for my dad and had saved some nice material for him. Uncle Fred was making a surprise for mother and had enough lumber to build a nice long table twice as big as the card table, and we would have enough room for our plates, and the food, and tea. Mother would love that because we now had to fill our plates in the kitchen and walk back each time for more bread and potatoes.

Also, he was building Mr. Doyle a chest for his sweaters and long underwear and a small stool for his feet. Mr. Doyle was a retired postmaster from our little post office where we walked for our mail. With our table and Mr. Doyle's chest and stool, Fred had three pieces of furniture to finish before December 25th.

Uncle Fred came home with a very small tree that we put in the corner near the front door. Of course, we made all our own decorations, and we stuck a photo of a magazine angel on a piece of cardboard for the top branch. Mother and I made popped corn so we could use a needle and white thread to string it for the garland. With some ribbon we made little bows for the branches, and the tree just looked splendid.

Christmas morning we had a real treat of homemade coffee cake on the new roomy table. It brought tears to my mother's eyes, and she was totally thrilled to have such a fine gift and have so much room. It did our hearts good to see her so happy on a Christmas morning. Certainly Fred was a fine craftsman, and one look at the table told you how much skill he had in his hands. We now could all sit in comfort and have room to eat, keep the food dishes, teapot, sugar and milk within reach as we enjoyed our meals.

My usual gifts were well received by me because I did not hope, or expect, to receive any expensive items outside of my candy, orange and maybe an apple. Mother surprised me with a lovely pair of red mittens she had knitted, and I knew I would be proud to wear them to school to show them off. I surprised Uncle Fred with a bar of chocolate candy. He seemed so happy when he unwrapped the paper. Someone had given it to me, so I put it away for him, though temptation almost made me eat it a few times. We had some white shelf paper, thus every gift was wrapped with the same whiteness and string, but in a way it was so striking we all felt that it was most unusual with the snow like setting under the little tree.

Uncle Fred tied a dishtowel over my eyes and told me not to peek. I sat with my hands folded on my lap wondering what he had in mind. There was movement and some scraping in the living room, and then suddenly Christmas music hit my ears, as the towel was untied from my head. There stood a large cabinet that said Atwater Kent on the face of it, and it was the best gift I ever received during the Great Depression, for Mr. Doyle had swapped it to Fred as an exchange for his chest and stool. As it turns out, Mr. Doyle was so deaf that he could no longer hear the music or voice, so never turned it on anymore. It was a wonderful sounding radio with a very large speaker that took up most of the bottom of the large cabinet. That was a wonderful gift in the hard times of unemployment and poverty.

The four of us sat at the long dining table and laughed and cried our way through the Depression while we drank our tea and ate our snacks. We were the audience to love, hate, crime, horror, and fun, all in our wonderful tiny living room with our ears tuned to the large cabinet. I had a sense of attachment to Sadie and the rest of the country when I heard the news, for before radio we had to depend on the newspaper. Even the President could now talk to us with his fireside chats. Here I was with the three people I loved most in the world, happy and content in our small West Texas town in the bad days of the thirties.

Flight

My husband pestered me for years to have children, but I was not getting tied down like some of my friends. My life was free of responsibilities so I could shop, go to the afternoon movies, and not have to worry about babies and diapers, and teenagers later in life.

My husband was a salesman and was away during the week with a territory that ran from Oklahoma to California. Thus, I was pretty much on my own most of the time and liked the arrangement. I had no desire to be pinned in a house with screaming brats.

Howard just phoned to say he would be home in an hour and was really hungry. This gave me enough time to bake some potatoes, heat some vegetables, and get some meat out of the freezer. He came in with a kiss on the cheek, and I sat with him while he started eating his salad. Oklahoma was a bit hot, but he made some sales, so the trip was productive. When he had finished, he asked if I had coffee ice cream, something I never bought, but I countered with some vanilla, which did not interest him. He decided to run to our little neighborhood store to get the ice cream and pick up his prescription. He said he would bring in his dirty clothes and suitcase when he returned, and did I need anything from the store?

While he was gone, I washed the dishes and checked to see if there was enough soap for a couple of loads in the washer when Howard gave me his dirty pile of shirts, socks and underwear. It was getting late and I phoned Dan's store to see if he was still there, and did he get his ice cream? Rose said he left a half hour ago, but did not buy anything but a doll and baseball glove and picked up his prescription. The toys were a puzzle to me, and I had to wonder why he bought them.

Well, it was now eleven, and he had left at seven, so I was worried that something bad had happened to him. So I phoned the hospital to see if any car accidents had come in or been reported. No, it was a slow night there, and when I phoned a missing person's report to the police station, they informed me they usually had to wait twenty-four hours before they filed it, and by then he would probably be home. Also, did we two have a fight before he left?

Well, the phone rang at ten in the morning, and it was Trevor Scott asking for Howard. I had to tell him he never returned from the store last night. He worked in the office with Howard and wanted to talk to him. When he heard he did not return from the store, he kept saying, "Oh dear, that is too bad." He seemed to be hesitating, like he had something to tell me. Finally he said, "I am so sorry, Thelma, but I am afraid I have to give you some bad news."

If he was phoning for Howard, and he was looking for him, what bad news was about to follow?

"Howard quit his job last Monday and turned in his sales slips and deposits, and the company property."

I said, "How could that be, since he was in Oklahoma?"

"Howard left his dirty work for me, and I phoned to talk him out of it."

"Out of what, Trevor?"

"Howard has been seeing a young widow with two children, a boy and a girl. He actually has been in town all week staying at her place while they have been packing. The four of them are leaving for California in her travel van and will be buying a house there. He will be leaving his car here for you, and from the window I see it is already in our parking lot."

Wow, I had to sit down at that news. This house was rented, and I immediately phoned the bank to ask the balance in our joint account. The girl informed me that nine thousand dollars was withdrawn three days ago, and the balance is now eleven hundred dollars.

Between sobs of sadness and tears of madness, my life fell apart in one day. I would have to pull myself together and survive on my own. That meant getting a job right away to keep up with the rent, food, and pay the gas, water and electric bills.

"Thanks a lot, Howard, I sure hope you enjoyed your dinner last evening, you fink. Also, how kind of you to share our banking account with nine thousand dollars for you and eleven hundred for me. I could ring your selfish neck, and hope I never see your dirty laundry again."

I used to be a nurse at the hospital in town. I still took courses to keep up with the new medical knowledge and enjoyed the classes, since Howard was on the road so much. Thank God I had something that I could use right away.

It took me a month to get in the swing of the hospital routine, and my poor feet had not traveled as much in years. Also, my afternoon naps were definitely history. Sometimes I pulled night duty, and that threw my sleeping clock out of kilter, but I had to hang in there so I could keep up with the bills.

Most of the days that I worked I headed for the cafeteria for a simple lunch, and usually waited until one PM when the crowds thinned out so I could grab a table. Yesterday they had my favorite meatloaf, and I was lucky to catch a two-chair table near the windows. The place was full, and a male voice inquired if he could sit in the spare seat. When I looked up, it was a nice looking doctor, and the fact that the place was full told me he did not seek me out. He truly just wanted a place to eat.

We talked a little bit of friendly chatter, and that was that. A week later as I pushed some peas over my tongue, that same masculine voice asked to join me for lunch at my table, and I took note of the fact that there were two empty places nearby. A meal together once in a while took place, and we talked a little longer each time. Six months of these hit or miss encounters led up to a dinner out on a Sunday night. This made me nervous because it put some pressure on me to realize it was an honest date.

He picked me up at my door and seemed surprised to see me all dressed up, hair done, and no nurse's white uniform or cap draped on my body. Frankly, I had the same reaction to his nice jacket with a white shirt open at the collar, and no hospital green outfit surrounding his nice hulk. A number of dinners and movies followed until we both were quite comfortable with one another.

We were now into the kissing game, but both cautious about a deep relationship as we walked slowly into our friendship. He had talked about marriage, but not in the sense of asking me, but more in hearing about me. I did not give out many details, and he just mentioned he was a widower and tired of the lonely life without female company at home.

Now we were casual with our comfort, and he asked me to a Sunday cookout at his home. He was going to cook burgers and hot dogs, and serve his own potato salad and coleslaw, plus some ice cream and cake. He would pick me up and personally take me to his door. He gave me a big kiss before he left my front hall, and it was longer and more potent than the previous ones. There was no question that I really liked this man and enjoyed his kisses and attention, and he seemed to be in tune with me also. He was a gentleman and a great catch for a husband, for his home was lovely as we pulled up to the circular drive. Out he jumped and opened my car door for me and led me into a big, well furnished living room.

He mixed me a drink and gave me a quick kiss as he took my hand and walked me out to the back patio. It looked like a convention at a boys' school, as seven young males lined up to meet me. He went through the introductions, and by the time he got to the seventh, and oldest, none of the names could I retain. They ranged in age from three to eleven, and I was overcome with the realization of his very large family. They all seemed nice, and we nine people downed our burgers and side dishes as they talked about sports and baseball. Can you imagine cooking and feeding this gang every day, to say nothing of the washing machine going steady night and day with seven pair of undershorts, shirts, and such?

When I got home my longing for this man was divided in seven pieces, and my desire for marriage flew out the window. In all the time I had known Dr. Kemp, he never mentioned his family, and with good reason, he saved the boy scout troop for the finale, and probably had gone this route before.

I grabbed my suitcases and threw the rest of my clothes in some garbage bags, and decided to try the nursing job in Tucson. My rent was paid up, and I phoned the utility companies in the morning and told the hospital that I had to leave right away for the Tucson hospital.

I dropped a music cassette in the radio slot as I pushed down on the gas pedal to drive my unsaddled spirit into the unknown future. Thank God, I was free again and cried out, "Arizona here I come, and that won't be soon enough for me." That sure was a close call.

Nebraska Homestead

My neighbor, Joe, was a fair farmer like me, but we had very little land with no possibility for acquiring more in our lifetime in our Massachusetts location. The plain truth got Joe talking about going to Nebraska and grabbing a homestead before the land was all gobbled up by Easterners.

Of course, we would visit over coffee and talk about it for months, until a friend of his dropped in one night to say goodbye. His train was leaving on Saturday for the plains, and he was expecting to pick up one hundred and sixty acres of prairie land by way of the Homestead Act.

Well, poor Joe could hardly stand this news, since that many acres to us poor dirt farmers with only a couple of acres sounded like pure heaven. That would be enough topsoil for an honest crop. Plus, we could keep some animals in one pasture.

We both decided to sell everything we owned, including the house and barn, to get enough funds for our adventure. We would need to buy a mule or pair of horses that could pull a wagon and plow, plus some tools once we got to the promised land.

It took us a month to hustle and settle our affairs, and I sold my place to a neighbor whose son was getting married and wanted the land near his father's farm since they both worked together. Joe lost some money on his house and two acres, but was so anxious to move he could not wait for a better deal. He had enough for train fare for his twin sixteen-year-old boys, wife, and farming necessities. His boys were big strapping fellows and could work all day without getting tired. They would help me with my sod house when they had some time from their chores and home construction for their family.

As soon as we landed in the town to get the Homestead papers, we declared our intentions to settle, farm, and meet the five-year requirements of the Homestead Act. We were directed to the locations of our side-by-side 160 acres, and Joe would get off to a good start with three strong men, whereas I would do most of my construction by myself, since I was a lone bachelor.

I put my little tent in the location next to where I would start digging the trench for the sod house foundation. I bought some lumber for a little lean-to barn for my horses and put that together before starting my house. I used a large spade to dig out the sod to the proper length, and I learned the thickness that would work the best so it would be stout enough for the walls. The horses and I drove to town to pick up bags of lime so I could mix it for the foundation stones that had to go in the trenches before I could lay the sod above the ground by a few inches.

The house would be longer than wide, so I had to dig into ground that had never been moved before. It was so hard, a pickaxe could hardly dent it, but I kept digging it out foot by foot with a rest every half hour until I could see some progress. It took me over a week to break that ground, so the stones from the creek would now be tossed into the wagon, as the horses could pull that weight alongside the trenches for the unloading. I put the lime mix in with the stones, and it seemed to set up hard and made a good strong base for the sod. Some farmers just set the sod right on the ground, but rain through the years would soften the dirt and lead to problems.

It was backbreaking work, and I had to get up early in the day before the sun rose to avoid the afternoon heat, which was very penetrating. The horses and I would wilt later in the day, so we took a rest then, and I put the team under a four-legged shelter just to give them shade. The wind could blow through it, and it served them well because they would walk right under it in the high temperatures in the afternoon. I rigged up some shade for myself and sometimes fell asleep after putting in so many hours from five thirty in the morning.

By early evening until dark, I kept at the sod cutting. I tried using the plow to break the dirt in even rows, so I could spade the turned earth into one-foot-wide sod bricks, and they would fill the wagon many times. The mosquitoes would plague us as the dark of evening approached, until we longed for the black of night to escape the swarms.

I had heavy anchors of stones tied to the hobbles on the horses feet so they could feed, but not stray from my vision. Once they were watered in the creek, they were hungry for grass, which was knee deep in every direction. I would give them each a handful of oats and let them feed in the abundance of green pastures.

Joe came over to see how I was doing with the house and

offered me his sons so we could get the roof over the structure. Their place was finished weeks ago with all his hands working together. The boys would finish my roof in a few days, and I finally had a good shelter over my head. Joe mentioned his sister Marie was coming to live with them, and they had addled a small room on the back of their soddie for her.

As a bachelor, my ears perked up, since I would love to meet a prospect for a wife. They would bring her over to meet me once she arrived.

My roof shed the thunderstorm rains while I worked inside getting shelves next to the sink, so I could prepare my simple meals. Then I built my chairs and tables, and a bed to make it home. A used cook stove with the pipe was purchased from a neighbor, so it could serve to heat the house and cook in the days to come.

I was into a dirty job one day when Joe brought his sister over to meet me. She said, "Hello," and I was impressed with her looks and shape, but I could tell it was not reciprocal as she seemed to be rushing Joe home.

After doing morning plowing and some seeding, I had installed the stove pipe for the stove and viewed the black soot on my forehead, and my shaggy, wild beard. My arms were also covered with a mixture of sweat and dirt, so my appearance was not too appetizing to a young girl.

A horse and buggy pulled alongside the house while I was outside washing, and it was my neighbors to the east of my spread. Vera and Ted Blake wanted to invite me to dinner the following night, and I was delighted. The next morning I took a bath in the creek, performed a one handed haircut in the mirror, and shaved the fur off my face. I viewed a good-looking man of twenty-nine years with muscles in both arms and legs that hard work produced.

Friends had told me the Blakes had three daughters, and they all but fell over me once I crossed their threshold. They did the cooking and serving and fed me like a king, until one more piece of pie would have struck me dead on the spot.

One caught my eye at once, for she looked to be about nineteen or twenty, whereas the other two appeared to be fourteen and sixteen.

Finally, I got enough courage to ask her to go to church with me on Sunday, and I would take a picnic lunch with me like some simple sandwiches, but she insisted on bringing the food, which gave me relief from that ordeal. Thus, I would pick her up in my wagon before the service and thanked Mrs. Blake, Mr. Blake and the girls for the wonderful meal.

When I got dressed up Sunday morning and walked into the church with Becky Blake by my side, I felt like a married man would feel, and proud to be with such a fine looking woman. Joe came in with his family and greeted me with a hello to the both of us, since he knew all the Blakes.

Joe said, "Marie, you remember Peter Powell?" She took a double look at me like I was a totally new person, and I got side looks and smiles from her all through the service. Becky seemed to notice this also and turned to look at her.

After the service, came the social time in front of the church as neighbors wanted to visit and talk about their crops and the weather. Joe came over to me while Becky was talking with a friend, and Marie was on his heels, as Joe invited me for dinner next week after the service.

Marie said, "I hope you can come."

I replied, "Thank you, but I'll be with Becky since I am now courting her."

Marie stepped backward a few feet, like she realized she was not too friendly upon our first meeting. Then it struck me that, had I been washed, shaved and dressed in my Sunday best when we first met, I probably would be courting Marie today instead of Becky, but Marie had made me feel like a grubby dirt farmer, which I guess I was.

Then I laughed to myself and realized how the grime gave me time to meet Becky, and how lucky I was to be caught on a day I had been working on the filthy stove pipe when Marie came to meet me. The fact is, Becky sent a shiver up my spine the first time my eyes saw her, and I knew this was the girl I wanted in my sod house. She was pretty, strong, a good cook, had a nice singing voice, and could stand behind a plow if need be. My honest working grime, and providence, had delivered me into the arms of Becky Blake, my future wife.

Route 93

Most of the planes were overbooked for the Christmas Holidays in the winter, and the drive was always a dice toss due to the unpredictable weather. I had seven last minute gifts all wrapped for my brother's tree in Elko, Nevada. That was where I was headed, since being an aunt to his swell kids was one of my great pleasures.

The morning was very cold, but clear, and the weatherman gave me a go ahead sign with his fine forecast for the next five days. I considered it a bit of luck at this time of the year, since usually the roads could be quite treacherous in December.

The car was packed with my bags, some snacking food, and the wrapped holiday gifts, plus a new digital camera I was going to try on Christmas morning when the kids unwrapped their gifts.

My drive toward Las Vegas was routine, but it always got interesting when I turned north off Interstate 40 and headed up Highway 93 into the long stretch of unpopulated country. It was a good route to Elko, but certainly not a major highway by any means. Thus, I always kept my tank on the full side and did not like to get the mark below half. Most towns were few and far apart, so I had a few favorite spots for my meals. The gas station and café were coming up in another hour, so my stomach looked forward to a good dinner there.

After I paid the cashier for seven gallons of regular, I walked out of the blustery cold December air and grabbed a small booth by the front windows, facing my car. The comfort of the heat in the small café made me a bit lazy, and the waitress took my order. She brought me a small steak with a baked potato, applesauce, and string beans. I immediately dug into my dish and was fully enjoying each bite when a strange hippie looking man of around thirty plunked down across from me on the opposite side of the table. He asked for a ride north, but I informed him I never picked up strangers and told him to try some man, or truckers headed in that direction. He gave me the creeps with his long greasy hair and shaggy, dirty beard.

Not even a trucker would want to share any close space with him. I asked him to leave since I was still hungry, and wanted to finish my dinner in peace. He continued to sit in my booth until I caught the owner's eye, and he came to my aid. I explained that the man would not leave my table, and wanted a ride. The owner was a nice looking gentleman, and he told him to move his carcass away pronto and stop bothering his customers. When I went into the rest room, I took my time and peeked out the door to make sure he was gone. Then I breathed a sigh of relief and was ready to resume the drive north.

I clicked my remote to unlock the door and slid behind the wheel of my car just as the passenger door opened and the greasy creep pointed a small Saturday Night Special right at my chest. "Back this car up right now lady, or you're toast." Believe me, the car jumped back, and I threw my gears into drive and flew up Route 93 as he kept pushing the gun in my ribs.

When we hit the desolate part of the lonely drive, he made me pull off the road and ordered me to move to the back of the car. He took my purse, grabbed all the bills out of the zippered compartment, and asked for the rest of the money. I had to tell him I did not carry that much cash and used my charge card when I was traveling.

He pushed me against the trunk, as he opened it with the key, and gave me a quick shove so I fell on the suitcase and Christmas gifts, and he slammed the lid tight over my scared body. He yelled that one scream, and I would be cold stone dead in the market. Thank heaven I had a warm jacket, for it was getting dark and very cold in the high desert air. I was shaking from fear and the cold, and because of the darkness could only go by the feel of things, and remembered the football stadium blanket I kept in the left hand corner of the trunk. I recognized the soft texture of the material and tossed it on my cold legs and feet.

As I fingered the small gifts, I searched frantically for my brother's box, which was in the bottom of the garbage bag with the rest of the boxes of candy, cookies, gifts, extra Christmas wrapping paper, and scotch tape. I fumbled in haste trying to feel the right size, for his was the smallest box. I expected the creep was waiting to find a lonely turn off up a dirt lane, so he could shoot me, steal the car, and leave my body for the packs of hungry coyotes that wandered the barren desert. I could not seem to get my hands on the small gift at the bottom of the bag due to the confining darkness of the enclosure. I was a prisoner alone with this repulsive stranger, and he was sure as hell going to kill me.

My hands were still running through the collection in the garbage bag when the car slowed down and made a right hand turn. Then we were on a dirt road, for stones were hitting the undercarriage of the car's body, and the road became quite bumpy.

As I raced to find my brother's gift, my fingers hit the smallest box under the collection of the whole Christmas pack. I pulled it up through the candy and cookies and opened the box in haste as the car's acceleration slowed to a crawl. I pulled out the Damascus knife with the turquoise inlay handle and quickly opened the blade.

I rushed to push the blade through the bottom of my pocket so just the handle would be handy to my reach. My arms were not that strong, but my legs muscles were like hard rocks from walking up and down the high hills behind my house, at a high altitude. When he pulled the lid open on the trunk, my legs came flying out with a strong kick, since I had cocked my knees back for extra power. He went flying backward and hit the hard ground. His gun went off, but he was in no position to aim.

As soon as he was halfway on his feet, the Damascus blade sliced him from his left kidney to a deep slash across his stomach. Since I personally had honed the blade to a razor sharp edge while I was sharpening my kitchen knives, I knew it was superior to any I had used in my slicing jobs on roasts and turkey. It was an expensive gift, and the best blade you could buy.

By then I had kicked the gun out of his right hand, which left him pleading for help and a doctor. I wiped the blood off the blade on a Kleenex and closed the knife so I could drop it in my pocket. The moon was low in the sky, but his figure was outlined on the ground with his hands on his bloody intestines.

As I walked toward the car, I turned and yelled, "Merry Christmas Creep," and clicked the key in the ignition and headed north for a store with camping gear, so I could buy a Swiss Army knife for my brother. If I could just stop shaking before I arrived in Elko, I could tell everyone it was the usual nice trip up Route 93.

Over The Limit

My friend, Dr. Chris Rand, was taking me to the birthday dinner for his friends, Sue and Brad Hammond. Her birthday was the nineteenth and his was the twentieth of June, and they always celebrated it on Brad's date of birth, because he was the king. He was full of himself and loaded with his own self-made man image and importance. Lord, did he think he was important, and like a ham actor, was on stage most of the time. If you think I was unimpressed, you are right on the mark.

There would be six of us for the birthday dinner at the country club, because their friends, the Lyons, always hung out with them, and Joe Lyons was his straight man who always fed his ego and played up to the big ham. Chris and I were invited for this big celebration, and, as my father would say, "hog wash," because it was just another excuse to show off with attention from the club staff and bring on the booze. We had to toast them with champagne, and I only held my glass up, and then we would sing happy birthday with the young waiters, so everyone in the club could see the big fuss and join in singing if they felt like it. Well, I did not feel like it, but I did not have much choice.

The headwaiter brought out the decadent cake on a table on wheels, and they had a doll of a young lady jumping out of the middle of the frosting, naked, and it was rather gross, but they just loved it. Chris winked at me, for he had good taste and felt the same as I about Brad, but Sue was a sweet woman. He was about to say something when his cell phone rang, and he had to go to the hospital, as one of his patients was quite sick. He thought he could get back shortly, and gave me a kiss on the cheek.

I was hoping to eat the prime rib dinner that was Brad's special request and get out of there early if Chris got tied up for hours. Well, I stuck it out bored stiff since they were into their serious drinking. Because I did not imbibe the stuff, listening to four inebriated people talking silly and killing themselves laughing over nothing set me up for a very dull evening.

It became late, and the party was over, so I offered to drive Brad's car if he would give me his keys.

"No one drives my new Caddy but me, and I am just fine."

I wish I had come by my bicycle, for I could peel off the five miles in jig time, and get home in one piece. I got in the back seat with the Lyons, and Joe was moaning a bit, as we headed into town. A few miles from home, Joe asked Brad to pull over since he was about to get sick.

Brad slammed on the brakes and said, "I'll shoot you if you barf in my new car."

That was my chance, because we were on the edge of town, and only a couple of miles from my place. Already the sidewalks were here, so I announced I was walking home for the exercise, and no one tried to talk me out of it. Frankly, Brad was over the middle of the road line too many times for my comfort, and when I had again offered to drive, he said, "Sit down, and don't be a nagging bitch."

Sue gasped, "Brad that is not nice."

He replied, "I intended it to not be nice."

I had only walked a few blocks when the red Cadillac came flying by me going fifty in the twenty-five mile zone. As I was getting near the Lyon's house on my way, I saw flashing lights ahead and heard the ding dong of the ambulance coming in my direction, and heavens, what a mess greeted my eyes in the Lyon's driveway.

Apparently, Brad was about to drive by their house by mistake when Joe said, "Here," and instead of going by it, stopping, and backing up to make the driveway turn, Brad turned the wheel and slammed into the big tree next to the right side of the drive. He made the turn, but of course was going much too fast, and the tree stopped the car from rolling over, but almost folded the back of the car into a U shape. The police got Sue and Brad out, since their doors popped open, but the fire department had to use the power arms to open the left-hand door in the back of the car. I saw the Lyons come by me on stretchers, and they were as red as the car. Sue had a brace on her neck and was unconscious, but Brad was saying, my poor new car, and finally asked about his wife. His eyes met mine, and he looked away instantly. I think he got my message.

The firemen sprayed the gas under the car and made us stay away in case it blew up, so I went on my way home to get my car and race to the hospital to find out if everyone was going to make it. Chris would be shocked if he saw his friends come into the back corridor on stretchers. I phoned his cell phone number and told him to get to the emergency room, that Brad and company were in an accident. He had no idea because he was still with his patient.

It was going to be a long wait, so I went to the coffee shop and got a cup to take to the waiting room. Hours passed until Chris put his hand on my shoulder and could sit down for a minute with a report. "Thank God you were not in that car."

But I had to tell him, "I was until I got out and walked home. Brad would not let me drive, and I decided he had much too much alcohol to be behind the wheel, so I left by foot."

The Lyons were both dead, and Sue had a broken neck with a severed spinal cord. Brad only had some broken ribs and fractured wrist and ankle. He'll have to get a lawyer, since he killed two people while driving drunk. Sue will be a paraplegic incapable of caring for herself, and totally helpless.

A year went by, and Sue was in her own home with twenty-four-hour care.

I would stop by and visit her, but never did we ever mention the terrible accident. Brad was in jail for ten years and received five years for each death for the DWI.

Sue could now talk with more ease and informed me that next week was her birthday on the nineteenth, and her daughter Judy was baking her a cake. It would be the first time in thirty years that she would celebrate her birthday on the actual date, instead of Brad's date of birth.

"I must have Judy send her father a nice card, with a photo of me looking at the cake."

I thought, yeah, Judy, make sure you get the wheel chair in the picture with your mother's lifeless legs and arms tied to the chair's armrests with gauze. I sure hope all the booze was worth ten years in jail for you, a wasted, paralyzing life for Sue, and forever eternity for your great friends, the Lyons. Happy Birthday, Meathead.

Strings

Walking out of the doctor's office, tears were running down my cheeks as people stared at me. No, I had no medical affliction, just pure joy hit me at two PM when the doctor said, "You are finally pregnant, Frances." Does anyone know what magic is in those words, when you have been trying to conceive a baby for ten years? Wait until I hit Barney with the news tonight, since he has started talking about adoption, and at 42 years old, I am about to be a mother, hallelujah.

Barney and I went right out and bought a crib, a mountain of diapers, and everything that would be needed for the baby's room including pink paint for the walls, because that's a color for little boys with rosy cheeks, right?

As soon as the doctor said, "Do you want to see if it's a boy or girl?" I cried, "Absolutely." We both looked at the screen, but it looked like a storm cloud I once saw before a tornado in Texas. The doctor pointed and said, male. Well, Barney celebrated like he had won the lottery.

When they put the baby in my arms in the hospital, I poured my usual bucket of happy tears all over him, and the doctor said, "Easy does it, lady, he can't swim yet." He was truly beautiful from his toes to his nose.

His first birthday came and went, and he had his fists in the birthday cake, and wasn't that cute. By the fifth birthday, it was no longer funny, any more than putting the cat in the toilet, pouring his cereal over the dog's head, or hiding mother's car keys in the garbage. I was forty-seven years old with a monster on my hands.

When he went to school, I had so many notes from the teacher, we could have wall papered the back hall. He put frogs in her desk, worms in the little girls' hair, and the dog had packed up his biscuits and moved under our bed. The cat had run away from home in self-preservation. Some older woman found him and read our tag with the phone number on it. She loved the little stranger, and I informed her she could keep him and thought, she has saved the little bugger from death by torture.

Well, the schoolteacher said little Tommy was very smart, and I thought, "What does she know? The little kid has a mother in menopause, so my judgment is altered." The teachers, and school in general, said "He was just too much to handle, and would you try home schooling him for a while, or until you find a school that could take him?"

Oh God, why didn't I just take the pill like some of my friends, just forget motherhood, and take up golf like the rest of my middle-aged girlfriends. They were having fun at the club, lunches out, and golf and tennis. I was having a stroke with junior, and trying to keep up with his lessons, but the little fellow knew more than I could teach him. Well, how did anyone expect me to know as much math, spelling, and science as this kid. After all, I had been out of school for twenty-some-odd years. Had I known God was going to call on me to home school, I would have paid more attention in class and gone for a B instead of my C marks all through grammar school. In high school, we had boys, so that took up most of my time, so I missed a few C marks and accepted a few D grades. Hey, who's perfect? I can read any comic book from front to back in an evening.

All this changed one afternoon when we left our kitchen table full of books that were over my head and walked to the park for a concert. Heavens, did I need a break. A young girl walked out on the bandstand with a big golden harp placed in front of her. Tommy would get restless, and squirm even in children's movies, because he could figure out the ending of the story before it took place on the screen, so got bored. I would ask him not to tell me the finale because it would ruin the picture for me. I figured he was good for ten minutes in his chair, but when this girl's fingers rippled across the strings, he was like the great stone face, frozen in time.

After the concert, he dragged me up to the stand, studied the instrument, and asked the girl if he could touch it. When he ran his hand across the whole row of strings, he smiled and even thanked her. When he got home, he begged me to buy a harp for him and pleaded with his father that he had to have one.

I told Barney, "I don't know what fascination or power that musical instrument has over our little devil, but whatever it is, if we have to mortgage the house and take in wash, we are going to get that kid back in his music trance for my own salvation."

Barney gave into the bag of strings, more for me than Junior, and the bank loan was worth every penny of interest.

Sunny put it in his room, and after he learned his way

around the octaves, we suddenly heard lovely music floating down the stairs. He came to the both of us, and said, "I think it is time for a teacher."

Did you ever try to find a man or woman that plays and teaches the harp? They are in New York at the music schools, certainly not in this one horse town in Kansas.

Dear God, what did we get ourselves into with this music business? You think a teacher is hard to find, try finding a new string for a bloody harp, and you are into a scavenger hunt. I never saw the boy cry until he broke that first string. But life had become so peaceful since the harp arrived from California that I was willing to steal a string out of the school piano at gun point if need be. Barney managed to get one on the computer

The boy was getting big now. So we thought maybe he could go to a music school in New York and advance to where his arrow pointed, wherever the hell that was.

He could hardly wait to go, and we did mortgage the house to send him. At his first concert, the critics declared that he was a genius. I turned to Barney, and said, "Oh for God's sake so that was his trouble, and I thought he was just a very backward child." Well, he was off on a concert tour sending his old mother and dad all kinds of money so we could pay off the house, buy us a new car, and get a sump pump for the foot of water in the basement. We were living high on the hog now.

Barney and I would laugh about the hell we went through bringing that kid up, and I reminded him of the time that he was so bad, I thought we had produced the devil. Barney had used a black ink marker, put 666 on the back of his neck, and said "Tell your mother to look under the hair on your neck. I think we have a problem."

I laughed, and said, "Barney, why don't we count our blessings. Our genius might have wanted a guitar, long hair, drugs, and women instead of a handful of metal strings."

"Well mother, that is true, and once when I took him to the band concert at the park, he fell under the same spell as the harp, and hells bells, he was infatuated with the damn tuba."

Montreal Awakening

Morgan was engaged to a witch, Molly; and even after he gave her a ring, she came on to me one night. I told him about it, because I hated to see him get hitched to such a non-loyal wench. He just said, well she probably had too much to drink, so he dropped it, and never thought it was that serious. What if it was some other lug who did not respect the fact that she was going to marry one of his friends? Well, I got so I disliked her so much, that I declined to be his best man, but he respected me for being honest, and it did not interfere with our friendship.

His parents and her family could not afford to help them out with the wedding, so Morgan was working two jobs, so she could have a custom wedding dress made for her hefty shape. It would cost nine hundred dollars, add that to the money for the reception, and you are talking real cash. That was my point, for if she truly loved Morgan she would not have him go into debt, work two jobs, and break his back just so she could walk down the isle to show herself off to her girlfriends. Besides, Molly did have a job in an office, but seemed to have her money tied up in some retirement plan, according to her, and could not contribute to any of the expenses.

Morgan's plant closed for two weeks to save money, and the part time job became full time work for some kid, so he was fired and worried about money.

I suggested a trip to Montreal, but Morgan said he did not have vacation money. J told him to relax, since we could take my little VW Beetle. It could get 34 miles to the gallon, and we could camp, make sandwiches in the car, and have a good time. Herbert wanted to come with us, and I swapped vacation time with a friend so I was free.

Herb was a nice fellow, but sort of a weak sister, and he irritated me at times because he was blind to so many things. First of all, he had a crush on Molly and stuck up for whatever dumb thing she did, and never seemed to realize how she took advantage of Morgan by spending so much money on the wedding and forcing him to pay for it all.

Anyhow, Herb's uncle had a burger place and gave us a bag of little packages of mayo, ketchup, mustard, and sweet relish, and would not let us pay for it. Now that does not sound like much, but we could go in a grocery store, buy a package of baloney and a loaf of bread, and make some tasty sandwiches. We each brought a blanket, a towel, and bar of soap, plus just one bag of clothes each to save room. We mostly wore shorts and tee shirts, so did not have to worry about a lot of duds.

The first night we pulled into the dirt road behind a small town park. There were johns, and a drinking fountain nearby, so we had a comfort station and a picnic table where we could sit and snack. It started to rain, so we got in the car. I got the back seat, so I could put my two pillows behind me and sit up with my feet across the two back seats and fall right to sleep. Since I had asthma as a kid, this was my usual position, so I still felt comfortable with my back against the side of the car and the pillows behind me. Herb and Morgan dropped their seat backs down and could stretch out, and I heard them snoring, so figured they were doing fine.

We got on the road early, stopped at McDonald's for coffee, made peanut butter and jelly sandwiches in the car, and were quite content. It got rather hot, so we needed a shower. We went to a regular campground that night and split the fee three ways, which was no financial burden. I was the first one to take my shower and took my towel in a garbage bag and the soap in a plastic lunch bag. I could leave my wallet and watch in the car with Morgan and Herb. When I was finished, I threw my wet towel in the dryer for fifteen minutes for a quarter, and it was ready for the next time. We would all do the same thing and could use the washer when we wanted to put our sweaty clothes and towels in the soap for a clean start.

We made Montreal the next morning, drove around the town looking at the sights out of a tour book, and decided to go to the Chateau Frontenac for a beer, just to see the lovely structure. That was quite a good move on our part, because we met two lovely girls from Connecticut on their vacation, and, boy, were they good-looking dishes, and nice. Morgan was having such a good time with the brunette that he was like a new man. She was really putting out a smile and eye flash for him. By the time we left, we moved on to another hotel with them, because by then we threw our frugality out the window and had a lovely dinner and dance.

Since Herb and I both had good jobs, we could afford to pay for the whole meal. We only did the cheap trip for Morgan's sake, else he would not have come with us.

When I saw Morgan with the pretty brunette, he looked happy for the first time in years, and he was like he used to be before Molly got her clamps into his wallet. The both of them seemed to be bonding with good chemistry. They were having so much fun kidding one another and just meshing that I knew this was the first time he ever had this rapport with a woman, and certainly never with mean Molly. Suddenly, I think he realized that he was led into marriage against his will and just sort of went along with it. Now he had different ideas about having a soul mate who was in harmony with him.

We three guys piled into a motel for the night, and we had a long talk on the subject. Morgan frankly said, "I don't want to marry Molly, because I have seen the other side of what it would be like to have a mate that really wants to be with me. As of now I have never enjoyed being with a woman as much as I have these past three days."

Herb did not utter one word, and he seemed to know enough to keep his thoughts to himself.

The girlfriend Barbara, with the brown hair, really appealed to me, so I was having feelings like Morgan, and we started to make plans to meet the girls in Connecticut, because it was close to New York, and we could take the train, or even drive that run. We had to leave Montreal the next morning, so I would be on time for work on Monday. Because of these two lovely girls, we hardly talked on the drive back, because Morgan and I had feelings we were kicking around in our brains. Herb was reading a magazine while I drove, so it was a peaceful trip until we hit the New York traffic.

Morgan and I were going to slip off to Connecticut as soon as we could, and it was no problem for me, but Molly was giving him a hard time about making some money for the reception and had added four more people to the list of fifty dollar a plate seats.

Nevertheless, we took the train to Darien and met the girls for dinner. By now we were making more dates and invited them to New York for a dinner and show, and Morgan just slipped away from seeing Molly by saying he had a sore throat. These back and forth meetings kept us busy, and pretty soon, my date Barbara and I got very romantic, and I was thinking, this is the gal for me, so I gave her a ring before some other guy got his foot in the door.

Morgan explained his problem to Sally the brunette, and told her he made a big mistake and was going to call his wedding off, even if she did not want him. For he now knew that his love for her was something he did not have with Molly. She was quite taken with him and felt that he was that special to her also, but unlike the witch did not want him to work and spend money on a big expensive wedding.

The four of us decided to fly to Vegas and get a quick wedding there. We'd enjoy all the wonderful sights, dinners and shows, Paris, and the gondola ride at the Venetian hotel and hit some of the fabulous buffets.

Before we left for Nevada, Morgan spelled it out to Molly, and she had a total fit and hit him with a vase. She cried about her wedding gown and was going to keep it, since it was all ready made for her, and Morgan had paid for it. The hotel contract stated it wanted a big cancellation fee, and on and on, and then she smacked him a hard blow with her rolled up fist, and he grabbed her by the hair, and said, "You are a witch."

We four had a double wedding and had a marvelous

time together in Vegas and stayed at the Stratosphere. We loved the rotating restaurant at the top of the tower, for the view at night was breathtaking, and the roast beef dinner was excellent. Barbara was so much fun that we four laughed our heads off.

We flew back to the Big Apple, and started to plan our future lives. Morgan's mother gave him a big check for a refund on the reception. Why, because dumb Herbert picked up the whole tab for everything if Molly would marry him. You don't think she was going to say no to that free lunch. She had a second chance to parade down the aisle in her nine hundred dollar wedding dress with her girlfriends looking on with envy. The fact that the groom was replaced was of no importance to her.

When Morgan and I got together, he burst out laughing and could not talk for a minute from the spasms as he bent over and roared, "Wait until Herb finds out she is pregnant, and believe me, I am not the father. He's the Chinese cook in the office cafeteria, and I just heard the news this morning from Molly's girlfriend. Because of the trip to Montreal, you saved my backside and delivered me from the wicked witch. You got me out of Oz ahead of the tornado, thanks buddy."

Under The Stars

Mother called the kids into the kitchen for the surprise she had for them.

"Well, kids you know we can't afford the trip to Disney World that we promised you because of your father's pay cut. If we start saving money starting tomorrow, maybe we can manage it next summer. The doctor said your father's indigestion is from stress, so he wants him to take a vacation. This year, we are going to introduce you to nature, the birds, the wild flowers, the stars, and the sky. We're going to take a camping trip to the National Park"

"Oh Mom, you make it sound so nice, the flowers, the stars the sky, how about the tics, the snakes and the hungry bears?"

"Your uncle is going to lend us his tent, and we can bring our own sleeping bags, towels, soap, and charcoal."

"And how about television, toilet paper, and video games for us kids, and do we have to go?"

It was settled. The two boys were in the back seat with the dog, Rufus, and we had the map in our heads and our eyes were looking north. Papa signed us into the camp and paid our fee for the car, where we were ushered into our reservation campsite. It was above the lake and a short walk to the water.

The kids wanted to go swimming right away and change into their suits, so we had to get working on putting up the tent. It was a lovely piece of nylon, and Ralph told the kids to help him.

"Hey dad, aren't we supposed to have little poles that slide in these slots to hold up the thing?"

Well, the poles were not there, and the kids had to change into their swimsuits. We took my clothesline, tied it to some trees, and ran the line through some of the loops on the sides of the nylon. It looked strange, but the tent was up, and the kids were swimming.

Ralph got the charcoal going in the little park grill that was anchored in a cement slab, and we brought some hot dogs in the cooler. The smoke was going in the tent because the location of the trees forced us to put the tent in the line of the fire. We closed all the flaps to keep it out, so we would not have to sleep in the wake of a barbecue pit. Of course by nightfall the smell was so bad that the kids moved into the car, and Ralph and I slept with the mosquitoes behind the car. That is, until the thunderstorm moved in. It's the first time I ever slept in a car with two kids, a smelly dog, and a husband.

We woke up to rain, and the kids wanted their breakfast. I made bacon bit sandwiches right out of the jar, and the kids were bored silly. "Didn't you bring some books to read? Can't you play some games?"

By nightfall, the smell in the tent was bearable, so we could flop on top of our sleeping bags and push the warm nylon away from our humid bodies, since the tent looked more like a thin shower stall instead of the original shape. Ah, the rain had stopped, and we had the charcoal simmering our nice burgers, and the kids were holding their rolls over the heat to toast them. The wind had shifted, so the smoke blew away from our sleeping quarters.

A roar came from behind the tent and bellowed over our peaceful setting.

"Oh my God, kids, get in the car right now."

We slammed the doors and locked them, and put our noses against the windows to watch the smart black bear knock the meat to the ground to cool it. He was not interested in us at all and first ate the rolls, and then devoured all our dinner that smelled so good.

"Get a picture of the bear Ralph."

"I can't, the camera is in the tent with the rest of the food."

"No it isn't, Dad, the bear just dragged it outside and is eating it right now."

"Oh Ralph, we are ten miles from the food store, and we are all hungry."

We gave up on the mess before us and decided we had no choice but to deal with it later. We got out through the park gate and headed for the town to get a bite and buy more food.

As we cruised along, a bumping noise hit our ears, and Ralph said, "Oh no, a flat tire."

When we got outside to check it, there was a broken whisky bottle someone threw out a car window. It shattered enough to leave some big pieces on the road in our lane. We got the car whiskbroom and swept it into the side weeds, so no one else would hit it, including us again.

The two boys started to move the bags out of the trunk

to get the spare from the bottom of the heap. Ralph could not find it, once everything was stacked in a pile along the road.

Our two boys, Ed and Dave, looked at one another, and when their father asked what happened to the tire that used to reside in the car well, Ed said, "Oh gosh, I couldn't get my backpack in the trunk, so I made room for it after I took the spare out and leaned it against the garage wall. I intended to slide it in sideways later, but forgot, sorry, Dad."

"Ethel, my indigestion is coming back."

It was the wonderful age of cell phones, so we were able to phone our emergency road service company, and they said as soon as they were finished with another call they would get to us, and where are you? Two and a half hours later, the truck arrived.

All we heard from the back seat was, "I'm hungry," and we still had to feed the dog. Everyone got a burger with fries once we got to town in the dark, and even Rufus got a cheeseburger and a few fries from the kids. We stocked up on some dog food, since once the bear dragged the bag around the tent and camping area, it was lost for a meal. We had to spend extra food money for Rufus and our own eating needs.

Once we got in the tent, we had to pull the small kibble and bits out of our sleeping bags, and Ralph had to take his stomach pills, so he could stop burping. I asked him why he ate the French fries. "Because I was hungry."

In the morning we were going to drive to the other side of the lake to watch the canoes paddle in the morning race. They were going to sell food there, and ice cream, so the kids begged us to go. We all jumped in the car and had our sunscreen, hats, sunglasses, and cameras.

"Let's go Pop."

But the car would not turn over, and Ralph looked under the hood to see what was the problem. The boys looked into the engine, and I looked into the engine, and Rufus stuck his nose in there, started sniffing like mad, and went into a barking fit. One of the nearby campers came by and asked what was wrong, since he heard the dog.

My husband burped and said, "The car won't start."

"Well, your dog knows the problem, and it is a common ailment here. Mice settle in the block when the motor is cool and chew your wires, and my dog has smelled them many times. If you have road service, they'll come out and find you if they know your location in this maze. They'll have to tow the car to a garage two towns away to find an auto shop."

Two hours later, the tow truck driver arrived after checking at the gate to see where our dead car was parked, and we had to wait for Ralph to come back with the car. We could not ride in our car, due to the insurance policy of the tow truck company, but the driver was kind enough to let my husband ride with him in his truck. It took an hour to get there, so Ralph could talk to the mechanics at Moses' Auto Repair.

When he landed at the garage, he got the extra bill for the tow because it was over the allotted distance fee. My poor husband had to see where our car was left so he would remember the location of the garage. Then he had to walk five blocks to a car rental office, pull out his driver's license, charge card, and drive back for the family. He burped for fifty miles and then faced us all with the news that we would have to pack up all our earthly goods and cram them in the back of the rental. We would now drive to this town where the garage was located and find out how long it would take to repair the engine wires. Then wait to know what the total amount of damage the mice did and how much it would cost.

Well, they always closed for the weekend, but they would get on it first thing Monday morning, and would take it from there.

Our vacation under the stars landed us in the creepy end of a bad neighborhood. As we all piled into the motel, the fellow at the desk said, "Keep your doors locked for safety and park your car under the street light near the front of the office."

The car was ready by Thursday, since they had to send for a part by express.

Finally, we got out of the motel, paid the bill at $100 a night for four of us, and extra for the dog. The shipping for the part was included in the garage bill, and by the time we figured up the motel, tow truck, and garage, extra food for the bear attack, and car rental, we could have stayed in a suite at Disney World. Ralph drove our car, while I got behind the wheel of the rental, and I followed him back to their office. We had to unpack the van, which cost more than a normal four-door sedan, since all the other cars were rented for the week. It was that or no transportation, so I guess we were very lucky to grab it. Then we all piled into our repaired vehicle and headed home.

There were a few extra stops the first day, because Rufus got car sick from eating a dead rabbit. Heavens, what a gagger, but we pushed on. My husband was tired, and the occasional gas cramp kept him from sleeping while I drove.

As the miles wore on, we approached home, and a loud burp followed by, "Are we there yet?" left Ralph's lips, and the kids started to giggle in the back seat.

Sally

My neighbor Sally was a cute gal around thirty years old. Her only fault was being a weak sister to her rat husband Mike. He was a control freak and put her under his thumb the moment she said I do. He gave her a charge card, and she could walk to a little grocery store three blocks away, pushing her little carriage, so she could tote her food home without having to carry it. She had a car when she married her slave owner, but he sold it because it gave her too much freedom.

Now she came next door to me, a divorced gal of fifty-five. She said she suspected Mike might be seeing another woman, because he no longer had breakfast at home and said he was working on getting the new promotion, so had to put nights in at the office. John Tully, who lived in the house on the other side of me, also worked for the same outfit and hoped to get the prized promotion, but always came home nights. Tully felt because he was fifty-seven, his chances were slimmer, but he was more civilized than Mike and certainly not as aggressive. This overbearing fault did turn people off, but because Mike was so cocksure of his good looks and fine physique, he thought he would mow down his competition.

Sally begged me to help her, and I told her she had to start telling this guy off and start standing up for herself. When her husband came home late three nights in a row, I said, "Come to my house before five o'clock," which was the office closing time. "Tully already told me that Mike was making a big play for the cute waitress across the street from the office in the Blue Diner."

We got in the old car my father left me, and I hardly ever drove it. We parked down the street from the diner and watched Mike's car park there for a minute until the redheaded waitress came out and slid in next to him. We stayed quite a distance behind his convertible and followed them to the movie house on the edge of town. When they both walked inside to see *Lovers And Killers*, Sally had a fit, because she begged her husband to take her, and he gave her a lecture on how selfish she was, when she knew he was working overtime at the office for the new job.

That was the turning point in her attitude about her lousy husband. We talked in the car until the movie let out and followed them to a swank restaurant. When they sat down near the big windows, he took the seat next to her instead of the opposite side of the table.

I rested my camera's long lens on the steering wheel and clicked every time he hugged her or kissed her on the neck, and it was often.

Sally suddenly had a little backbone, and started saying he was about to be her late husband. When he finally paid the bill, they headed to the end of town on the highway.

My old car had trouble keeping them in sight, but when he looped into the motel there, I continued past the place, so it would not look like anyone was following his car. When we came back, I parked across the street and took a photo of the motel sign blinking in the bright neon green lights. Their security outdoor lights were fine, since I could photograph his car and even make out the license number.

We drove home after that, and she said, "I would give anything to fly to Iowa and be on the farm with my mother and father. Mike would never give me money so I could visit them, and I feel trapped here."

I told her she was not stuck at all. She did not even have a suitcase, but her husband had a new lovely one with the wheels and zipper compartments, so I encouraged her to use it and grab her clothes after he left for work.

As soon as his car pulled out of the driveway, she came over with the full suitcase, which I put in my laundry room.

We then drove to my travel agent. She said, "I have no money," and I reminded her of the charge card, since she only ever could use it for food. Mike went over every item to make sure she did not buy any clothes or bathroom articles, since he picked out her outfits and needs about every six months.

There were two flights a day that connected to Des Moines, but the first one was too early and the afternoon one was at two-ten. She gave the girl the card and was informed, in order to get the discount savings, you had to buy two weeks in advance. There were a few empty seats on tomorrow's flight, but it would cost a hundred dollars more.

Sally said, "Good, and give me a first class seat if you have one at any price."

In the evening I printed the photos on my little printer and, when they were dry, put them in a small album I had in my desk drawer.

When Sally came over early in the morning to just get away from the house, we sat and had coffee and looked at the pictures.

She put them in her purse, and said, "When the time is right, I'll send them to Mike, just so he'll know I am not as dumb as he thinks."

Tully told me that he talked to the redhead when he ate breakfast in the diner some mornings, and she was engaged to a lieutenant in the army. As soon as he returned from duty, they would get married and move to his next assignment in Nevada. Also, she seemed crazy about him, so had been biding her time with a movie, free dinner and a little love on the side. Sally was happy to hear Red was not planning on Mike for a future husband and was sure he had no idea she was engaged.

I took her to the airport and went inside with her so she would not chicken out and turn around and go home. I slipped her two hundred dollars for extra money just in case of some emergency, but she reminded me that she had the card and invited me to lunch. We both ordered the most expensive meal on the menu and laughed when she handed the waitress the Visa card. She was that mad at him, and maybe she would buy some clothes in the airport shop. She chuckled and asked me if I would like a new car.

When I got home, Mike phoned and asked if Sally was there, and I told him, "I think she was going to the grocery store and wanted some onions."

He said her little portable carriage was still in the kitchen.

I said, "For a few onions, she probably did not need it."

When he got home late that night, she was gone, and her note said, "Thanks for the suitcase and airline ticket."

She phoned me to say she was so happy to be home with her folks and had informed them of her prisoner status as Mike's dumb wife. Also, she told them what he was doing with the girl in the diner and how mean he was to her. She thanked me for giving her the push she needed, and her joy in using the charge card for herself for the first time since she was married. She was sending me the two hundred dollars right away.

Her old boyfriend from school saw her in church that Sunday, walked over and sat down next to her. He was always so kind to her, and they were expected to marry, but Mike was a new handsome face and swept her off her feet, so she made a fatal mistake and married the slave master.

When Mike got the divorce papers, he said, "To hell with her, she'll come home and beg me to take her back. I have no fear of her staying on that dumb Iowa farm."

When he went to the diner, the redhead was gone, and he asked if she was sick, only to learn that she was getting married in Nevada and was about to live at her husband's new base. He was absolutely stunned, and then shock hit him on top of that when Tully got the new promotion. He left the office, saying he was coming down with the flu. When he got home, there was a brown envelope from Iowa in the driveway mailbox. "Ah, the girl has come to her senses, and it's about time, Sally, as I am getting tired of cutting the lawn, washing the laundry, and food shopping."

As he opened the album and saw the pictures of the redhead with his arms around her shoulder kissing her neck, his face became red. Then he turned the page and saw the photo of Red and himself walking into the motel door marked number five, and the name of the place in neon lights on the sign. The photo of his car parked in front of the door with the license number visible made him squirm. There was an envelope inside, and he tore it open to find a newspaper clipping with Sally and her new husband, Clyde Hopkins, just before they were about to fly to Paris for their honeymoon.

He studied the photo of Clyde, and decided he was an ordinary hick from Iowa and was no match for his good looks and build. Then he started reading the article on the Hopkins' wedding, and the large reception with two hundred people at the country club. Clyde was a Yale graduate and now the president and owner of the Marble Resorts in five states and the island of Maui.

"She is a little fool. It won't last, and she'll come crawling back to me. Sally, why would you do this to me?" He sat down over her little food carriage and started to cry uncontrollably as he kept saying, "You know you are the only one I ever loved."

St. Croix

On the island of St. Croix we used to help our friend, Adam, catch his tropical fish so we could put them in heavy-duty plastic water bags and get them to the airport for the evening flight to New York. Some of the fish would command a very high price, and the checks from the Big Apple would keep Adam in good cash for his simple needs.

Trying to hook these little tiny devils with a fish net was almost impossible, for they would dart out of reach in a flash. We only had one vacuum gun among the three of us, and I loved to use it on occasion. It contained a large plastic bubble on the end, and when you pulled the vacuum pump backward, a large volume of water would be sucked into the large container on the end. When the little fish got caught in the backward flow, you had them.

After we stored our catch, we would sometimes down some beer at the King Christian on the wharf and talk some guy talk on sports and women. One night while we were sipping and chatting, Adam got up to go to the men's room when he bumped into big fat Jake, who was a mean drunk when on shore. He had a fishing boat, *The Sea Dragon,* that supplied his catch to the hotels and food markets. Adam apologized and started to move away, but Jake grabbed him by the neck and gave him a punch on the side of the head. Well, in a minute we had a fistfight going, as they both knocked our table over, drinks and all.

We broke it up quickly, but Jake pointed his finger at Adam's face, and said, "You're dead."

A week went by, and the incident was mostly forgotten until we heard a loud voice yelling over the steel drums, and a shoving match was taking place against the wall in The Hamilton House Restaurant. As we stood to see who was behind the loud noise, I could view one of the local natives, Albert, getting hit on the face as Jake was hammering him with his right fist.

His last words were very threatening, as he finished with, "You're a dead man."

I turned to Adam and told him to be careful of this guy, because I did think he had some mental problem when he enjoyed fighting over small things and telling people he was wishing them dead. Alcohol did not help his ugly disposition, and when we walked out the door, Jake stood near the open entrance and slid his fat foot before Adam's leg, tripping him to the floor. We heard, "Your days are numbered," from the fisherman's lips, and we had to grab Adam away from him and drag him out the door to keep them both from fighting.

We happened to be talking over a coffee and muffin at Rasmussen's restaurant, when Josh mentioned that Albert was missing from home for over a week now, and his wife and kids were asking friends to help them find him, or give any information that might shed light on his whereabouts. Josh mentioned the fight in Hamilton House, and we all agreed that maybe Jake dealt him some of his crazy revenge.

On the weekend, I could not find Adam anyplace, and

we three were set to snorkel off Buck Island for the New York outlet, since their supply was running low. The car was still parked next to his shack, and when I looked in the window, all the paraphernalia was there. From his bedroom window I could see his bed had not been used, and no one in town had seen him since last night. We hurried to the police station and reported him missing, and they said they would put it into the usual channels including the local paper.

Three days later, the police phoned to give us the sad news that his body was washed up on the rocks below the radio station. His clothes were found on the beach, and he apparently went swimming in his under shorts. This made no sense to us, for how did he get to the beach without his car, and he would never go swimming in his under garments. We always took the little rowboat to stash our fishing items and anchored it near where we were snorkeling so we could put the caught fish in the plastic water tank. Adam certainly would not be swimming alone. We insisted that foul play was involved and wanted an autopsy. Jake's name flashed across our thoughts because Albert disappeared such a short time ago, and they both had threats from the same man, Jake.

Once the autopsy came back with the cause of death as the venom of a sea snake bite, we both said, "No way." Never in our knowledge of sea accidents did we ever hear of anybody getting bitten by one of these snakes while swimming in these waters, and that took in tourists and native reef fishermen. The sea snake is non-aggressive and always stays out of reach when we are underwater. I don't think many men could catch them with a net on a good day, and who would want to try?

Josh said, "Let's get the vacuum gun and see if we can

suck one into the holding chamber just by chance to see if it is possible."

Adam's full fishing gear was always in the back of his car, and since the car was strangely unlocked, we went in the shack, and the door had been jimmied. We looked to see if the car keys were on the nail near the door. No, they were not there, or anywhere, for Adam always put them in just that place. When we looked in the car, all the fishing equipment was spread around in little piles, from the goggles and rubber air hoses to the nets, plastic water bags and feet fins. The one thing that was missing was the vacuum gun. We looked at one another and decided to borrow our friend's gun just to see if we could catch a snake over the reef. We had a tough time even getting near one, but managed to vacuum a snake into the bubble in two hours. It did not want to get anywhere near us.

That night we decided to sneak down to the room on the wharf where Jake stayed when he was in town. His drunken pal actually lived there, so we had to sneak to the open window and check the room to see if he was out. After we dropped from the sill into the empty mess, we checked every nook and corner and found a very large insulated foam ice chest full to the top with greenish water. When I dipped my finger in it and ran it by my tongue, I realized it was salty, and I knew it came from the sea. When Josh found our vacuum gun, he recognized the dent on the nose that was put there when I banged it into the car door one day. This was definitely Adam's property. We put it back where Josh found it and sneaked out the way we came in.

I told Josh that I was pretty sure Jake caught a sea snake with the gun and put it in the large cooler. Then he and his friend grabbed Adam, dragged him into this shanty, tied him up. They most likely shoved his left arm in the seawater and poked the snake with a stick until he bit Adam's arm. Then they just undressed him, left his clothes on the beach, and took him out of the harbor in the dingy and cast him overboard.

We looked for the return of Jake's sloop. It drifted back into the harbor a week later, and while he was out boozing with his buddy, we swam out to his little boat with a waterproof flashlight, ruler, and a very fine drill bit with a handheld drill.

Josh measured the thickness of the plank siding by putting a tiny drill hole under the railing. It would never be noticed. He ran a small picture-framing nail through it five times, and I held a small wood match box against the siding where the end of the nail would come through the hole. Then his fingernails held the other end, and he kept measuring the thickness until each time it registered the same mark. Then we did the same operation to the dingy, until Josh was convinced he had the wood thickness to the mark.

Once back in our small beach house, he put the measurements down on paper and used his micrometer to get the absolute correct thickness of the wood planks. With an old drill bit, he worked on cutting it down to just that depth, so it would be the thickness of the siding. Then he moved to the next stage and filed enough millimeters off the length of the bit until he thought the depth was just right for his plan.

We swam back in the cover of darkness and used our oxygen tanks this trip.

Now we both got under the bottom of the boat while I held the flashlight as he started drilling plugs out of the hull boards, and the measurement kept them from doing a complete hole below the water line. He drilled them from one end of the hull to the other and left a thin fiber of wood to keep the water sealed.

We moved to the dingy with the same operation, carefully making enough dents in the bottom to satisfy Josh. Then we put the tools back in the burlap bag, kicked our rubber fins, and headed away from the vessel as our tanks were almost out of oxygen. We were tired and would rest for the weekend.

Monday morning, we rose early to watch Jake's *Sea Dragon* lift its sails and slowly catch the whiffs of the trade winds as it moved out of the harbor entrance. We held our breath as the sloop hit the small waves near the reef on either side of the channel. She was holding her own, cleared the mouth as it passed the lighthouse radio station, and headed in the direction of St. Thomas. It kept drifting into the horizon as it turned into a small speck in our binoculars and disappeared out of sight. We looked at one another with relief, since it could have sunk before our eyes. The rough sea was coming up, as the open waters were always quite choppy once away from the island.

A week went by as we waited to see if the sloop would return on its usual schedule. Then two weeks passed, and no *Sea Dragon* entered the harbor, until finally after a month we thought she was in Davy Jones' Locker for sure.

Our revenge for Adam and Albert was complete. Josh figured we saved some lives from that sick mind with Jake off the island, since he took such pleasure in fighting and threatening men he really did not know. Josh reasoned the taxpayers would not have to spend thousands of dollars for his food and board in jail if he was convicted. There was a chance he would have escaped a sentence, so we did not want to give him that opportunity, out of our respect for Adam. As it turned out, his few bum friends thought he went back to his own island of Puerto Rico to fish in his home waters, and we figured his Puerto Rican friends thought he had stayed in the Virgin Islands fishing for the hotel and markets. After a short while, his name never came up in any island conversation.

We decided Adam deserved our loyal friendship, since he was such a good honest person and a fine true friend. Had we been in the West, Jake would have been hanged or shot a long time ago. Our guilt and knowledge of the deed let us both drift off the island to the mainland, and we purposely lost contact with one another. We knew we would both think of our last days here, and our revenge, but we knew sometimes man must make his own justice, and we were the ones called upon to be the men.

Sparks

When Flo asked me to walk with her early every morning, I was happy to have the company, and this gave us a chance to have some good talks on our hike. We treaded north because the sidewalks went uphill, so we figured that extra effort would be good for our waistline.

Always, Mr. Collins would meet us coming from the other direction, and once Flo introduced me, he always said, "Good morning Flo, good morning Blair," and he sometimes chatted for a few minutes as he passed. Since he walked by Flo's place, he would comment on her lovely flowers and the rose bush against the house.

We stayed faithful to our exercise, but Mr. Collins suddenly did not appear on our trail at seven anymore.

Flo mentioned that her husband also worked at Cliffton Enterprises, and Vince Collins was one smart fellow because he produced many small patents for the company though the years. He had a little workshop in a back alley in town, and her husband once delivered something to him from the office and was fascinated with his tools and mechanical wonders. Collins told him his wife never seemed to be interested in his work, and started stepping out on him since he went to his shop many nights to work on some project.

His boss was divorced and was making a play for his wife, Alma, and he had caught them together in a closed office at the Christmas party. They were mauling one another, and the boss was tattooed with her lipstick. She asked him for a divorce a month later and told him to move out of the house, since she wanted to stay there alone. Her bad temper erupted when she heard he had mortgaged the place so he could pay a patent lawyer for a new quick charge battery idea he had invented.

I was interested in his battery idea, because mechanical things always caught my eye as a kid. When I wanted to take mechanical engineering in college, my folks had a fit. "Women don't become engineers, you'll have to pick something feminine and ladylike." So I hit the books and just took a liberal arts course, and ended up totally bored for four years.

When I went to the post office Saturday morning, I could not find a parking space due to the Christmas rush of people with packages. There were fifteen people in front of me with more than one box in their arms, so I just slipped out of line and walked back to the little café where I would sometimes have breakfast on weekends. As I slid into the booth, the waitress was right there taking my order of bacon and eggs, and toast and coffee.

When I heard, "Hello Blair, may I join you," my eyes fell on Mr. Collins.

I told him Flo and I missed him on our early morning walks, and we settled into a long conversation. When I mentioned how frustrated I was when I could not pursue engineering, he fell into a most interesting talk on his latest battery project. When I seemed to understand the basic principles of his idea, he invited me to come back with him to his nearby shop. He now was living there and had a small partition where he had his bed, and the place did have a shower and john. His boss found it awkward to have him in the same office now that he was pursuing his ex-wife, so he just plain fired him

Since he lost his job, he no longer could pay the mortgage on the house, so Alma moved into the boss's large home, which was the original plan, he thought.

His patent was being held up because Vince still owed the lawyer ten thousand dollars. It seems that a battery fully charge in a new electric car would take you about forty miles before the battery power was exhausted. Also you would have to keep it plugged into your garage outlet for eight hours or the whole night. Vince had come up with a revolutionary power unit that would carry you just under one hundred and fifty miles on one charge. That was a breakthrough in battery power for car propulsion, but the major improvement was the fact that it could take a full charge in forty-five minutes.

Now he figured that, in a couple of years, he could boost it up to a fifteen-minute charge, and a three hundred and twenty five mile range. Picture yourself on a trip across the country, and your battery dial shows you only have twenty miles left on your charge. You pull into the gas station that now has a solar electric power source that will plug into your car, and charge it fully while you sip a cup of coffee. A small buzzer in your hand will light up and tell you the car is fully charged and ready to roll again after only fifteen minutes.

Well, my ears were burning with excitement, and I explained that my aunt had left me twenty thousand dollars in US Savings Bonds, and would he consider letting me cover the ten thousand for the patent lawyer, and he could pay me back with whatever interest he deemed fair. He was thrilled that I had that much trust in him, and he would not only pay me back with interest, but give me thirty percent of the invention profits. Thus, if he could sell it to one of the major automakers, he would have a future retirement plan, and he could build a new house and shop in one structure.

Well, Alma showed up at his door and complained that the boss had a new secretary who was making a big play for him, and she was ten years younger than Alma, without one wrinkle in her face. Since she already had a few around her eyes, with some gray hairs in her blonde locks, she sure was mad at him. She threw Vince a pitch about moving back with him. He had to tell her he was living in his shop and really no longer was interested in residing with an ex-wife, especially since she could hardly wait to divorce him and move in with a lover.

"Well, you can always live with your mother, though you never gave her five minutes of your time and did not even invite her for Thanksgiving or Christmas dinner. Maybe she does not want you either, and now I have to get back to my work, so goodbye Alma. Oh, and thanks for getting me fired after twenty years of loyal service at Cliffton Enterprises."

I was quite relieved to hear that Vince gave her the boot after she left him and came begging for a return match.

Life has a way of striking back at you, and the boss was so busy enjoying the good life of wine, women, and rich food that his weight climbed to a disturbing poundage, and the new girlfriend said goodbye and moved on to a good-looking salesman who would pick her up from work at night.

When the boss had a stroke, it affected his speech and

movement on his left side. He could no longer hold a pen in his hand and function in the office, or on his own. His retirement took care of the nursing home for his future years.

Vince phoned me with excitement in his voice, and said, "I am going to take you to the Lookout for a special dinner tonight, so be ready at seven."

We had a nice view of the city from the outdoor patio. The lights sparkled in the warm dry air of the Southwest. Vince kissed me and said, "Here is your loan of ten thousand dollars, plus the interest," and handed me a cashier's check in that amount. Then he put an envelope in my hand and said, "Open it."

Another check sat in my hand with the numbers three million dollars typed across the amount line. "That is your thirty percent profit on your investment for having faith in me."

"Now that I have the seven million in my bank account, I am not ashamed to ask you to marry me, though it was on my mind for a long time. A man likes to have security to offer to the woman he loves. The auto company that bought the patent also offered me a job to perfect the later models if I can boost the mileage the new battery can produce and cut the time for the battery recharging. I know I can develop it and have it working in a few years with you by my side."

We then walked inside and let the headwaiter lead us to our table in the corner next to a window that had a different view of the lights in the distant hills. A waitress dressed in a black short skirt asked us if we wanted a drink, as she put the menus on the table.

Vince looked up and said, "Alma, I thought you were living with your mother in Phoenix."

"No, she married a snowbird from Chicago and went back with him to the windy city for the summer. Well, Vince, if you can eat here in a new blue suit, I guess you are doing all right."

Vince introduced me to her and said, "This is my future wife, Blair, and we are about to have a honeymoon in Hawaii in the next few weeks. That dumb battery I was working on that you hated because I could not take you to the movies paid off in spades, ten million dollars worth. Now excuse us, for I just remembered that my favorite prime rib is at the Ritz Carlton. Here's a tip for your time."

He dropped two dollars on the table. Like a general that had just won a major victory, he threw his shoulders back and stood to his six-foot-one carriage and marched to the door in triumph.

I turned my head and caught the expression on Alma's face, and it said, "There goes my ten million dollars."

Blanco Mountain

We had hiked clear to the mountaintop and took in the view of the aspen groves below us. The far-off mountains said wilderness, and the distance from civilization gave me a slight fear of my remote location from security.

Vic was a good devoted hiker and left me in the dust with his long stride. He was six foot four, and I was a five-foot-four woman, so I had to hustle to keep up with his long step. He sometimes got out of sight in the many trees, and I would have to call his name so we would not get separated in the dense foliage. There was no trail up here, and no guiding path to follow, since most people would hike in more popular locations.

Vic liked Blanco Mountain and decided to walk us down the steep backside of it on the north side. The plan was to slowly descend this steep course, until we got to the level ground at the base and work our way east until we could spot the two hills called Mother and Father. Once we could see them both, we would pass between them toward the green valley and get back to his Jeep.

We stopped for lunch, and we each carried our own supply of food. My friend Warren had made me a little hiker's stove out of soda cans by cutting two of them in half and putting one in the other with the two bottoms on each end. He cut the inside of one end to leave the rim and drilled holes in it. Once you poured alcohol inside and lit it, the fumes between the sides would turn to a blue flame and make a hot fire. I had a flat piece of thick tin that bent into a circle to place over it and support my pot of water.

The quick-cook noodles heated up, and I could add the cheese and a small tin of corn beef, so my stomach was well fortified for the hike from twelve thousand feet to two thousand. Lunch was done, and we packed up our gear and slung our backpacks over our shoulders, and started walking down the north side.

It was hard on the knees with our weight and our necessary packs, and I fell behind Vic by some distance. I presumed he was following a straight line, so I just followed his footprints when I could see his impression on the ground. After a short time of this workout, I yelled to him for a rest stop. I had mentioned this only ten minutes ago, and he had replied, "Good idea."

Now I yelled, "Let's rest now," and said, "Stop and wait for me." I kept coming down lower and yelled his name. There was no reply. Twenty paces more with his name at the top of my lungs again brought no response. Fear hit me in my shaky knees, and I studied the ground for some sign of a hiking boot print.

The smart thing to do was not move too far from this area and scan the ground first to my left, and then to my right, in case he veered from the straight line toward the base. My voice was hoarse from yelling, though it was more like a scream of panic.

Alone, I sat on the ground with my back resting against a tree and was there for the afternoon, afraid to leave the location in case Vic was looking for me. I stretched a nylon cord between two trees and hung a thick plastic sheet over it. Rain was starting to fall, and I used my knife to cut a slit on each end of the plastic. Then I could pull them together with clothespins. This arrangement kept me dry, and I curled up in my light sleeping bag to wait for morning. Not much sleep could conquer my fears, for the nighttime darkness produced visions of bears to mountain lions.

Morning found me in a sea of white snow, and I was afraid to leave and afraid to stay. The fact that I was alone and frozen with fear got my juices flowing, and I had to give myself a pep talk to pack up my things. I shoved the stove and sleeping bag into the pack and had to shake the snow off the plastic sheet, since I knew I would have to depend on it again very soon.

Trying to get my bearings was difficult in the white world, but I reasoned that walking down the mountain would eventually land me at the mountain base and flat, level ground. I would turn right, which would bring me near the foothills, and by then the visibility would allow me to pass thought the hills and lead me to the valley and vehicle. Vic might get there way ahead of me and wait there.

Instead of resting and cooking some food, I munched down some nuts and raisins I had put in sandwich bags. My God, my legs ached, for I just kept pushing myself down the steep incline and could not see the uneven ground before my step due to the slippery snow. The plastic sheet was a lifesaver because some light snow was still falling, and I had to lie down. My tin frying pan acted as a shovel as I dug out the snow under the nylon cord in the trees. I had to dig down to the dry earth to put my sleeping bag sheet on a dry spot. The nuts and raisins were not going to cut it for energy after all my physical labor of hiking in pretty deep snow. I was hungry, scared stiff, and totally bushed from my effort. Still, I had not made the mountain base as yet.

A package of freeze-dried stew was dumped in the frying pan, with the melted snow for water. I was too hungry to cook it hot and started eating it out of the pan with a spoon when the temperature was just a bit warm. It was so good, I ate it down like a starving dog. In a restaurant, it would barely pass for food, but at this moment of hunger in this lonely setting, it was like a plate of comfort in a four star restaurant.

My exhaustion put me right to sleep, and the howling wind in the treetops never reached my ears. The snow kept the plastic from blowing around my camp, and I had put a fair amount around the edges to weigh it down so the wind would not whip it off me during the night.

In the morning, the weather was down to a drizzle of rain, and I hated to leave my warm, dry sleeping bag. Breakfast consisted of some jam and crackers. My feet stumbled down Blanco's steep terrain, and by lunch I was tired and hungry. The crackers did not stick to my ribs for more than an hour, so I had been working on low energy power. A snack of chocolate and nuts perked me up, and I would cook something this evening.

If Vic made it to level ground, his cell phone would not work, since he could not pick up the signal until he reached the valley. I chose not to bring mine, since one phone between us seemed to be enough. Perhaps he would get to the valley way ahead of me and phone for help, since he would realize I was probably lost behind him.

Finally in late afternoon, I hit the level ground below the mountain and made my right turn. My tiny compass hung on my knife's key chain and pointed east, so I felt my direction was now correct. The visibility was still poor with a light rain and some fog. The hills were the key to finding the valley. If I missed them, my path would take me into deep wilderness, and I could find myself in no man's land. It was crucial to turn south between the Mother and Father hills.

My feet were wet and cold, but my breath came easier in the lower altitude.

The fog made me nervous, for I could not see more than a hundred feet in front of me. Fear of walking by the hills made me stop and kill time, hoping the weather would lift. My hat and jacket were waterproof, so outside of my wet feet, the rest of me was dry.

I searched in my pack for more jam and crackers and decided the fog was not going to dissipate anytime soon. Thus, I set up my sheet and got under cover and sat on my sleeping bag ground sheet with my back to the tree while I munched on odds and ends in my food bag. The fog was hanging on, and I was uncomfortable until I spread out the sleeping bag and curled up for the night.

In the morning, I fired up the alcohol stove with a can of beans, so my breakfast gave me some cheer. When the sun came out, the fog evaporated by the time I was packed up and ready to move. When I found a clearing, I was very happy to discover I could see between both hills. Had I kept on walking east, I would have missed the turn to the valley.

My hope lifted as I passed Mother Hill to my left. When I finally had Father Hill to my right, my spirits rose with each step. By late afternoon, I could see the white reflection of Vic's Jeep parked beside the off-road trail. It hit me that he did not make it out ahead of me, and I worried that some harm had stopped him, but he could be sleeping in the Jeep waiting for me. If not, the thought of a bear attack had crossed my mind, and my brain started to wander into tragic scenes until I had to turn off my imagination.

He was not in the Jeep, and not within yelling range, and it struck me hard that I could not access the vehicle without a key, since Vic carried it in his pocket. I could not drive it to safety and get a search going for him until I made it back to the highway and could get to a phone. Thus, I stayed on the tire tracks in the mud, knowing that the old dirt road to the highway was eighteen miles away. My bones were tired, and my downcast thoughts were no comfort to me as I sat against a tree for a spell. What had happened to Vic? flooded my brain until sleep captured my weak condition, and my weary body succumbed to nature. I fell over and stayed in that position until early morning. When I woke up, it was just starting to get light, and some stale crusts of old bread tasted good with the end of my jam. The food got me on my feet, and I walked the Jeep path until I made the dirt road by early afternoon.

Now the walking was easier, and I felt happy that I knew where I was, and that this next long walk would get me closer to the highway.

Suddenly, a loud motor noise came around the bend as two motorcycles appeared in front of me. I practically threw myself at them as I flagged them down. I told them my story and begged for a ride to a phone to get a search party on the mountain for Vic. One of the boys pulled out his cell phone and reported him missing. They were so nice and kind and gave me a ride directly to my home, but the ride at breakneck speed sitting over the back wheel was almost as scary as finding myself alone on the mountain.

The search party and helicopter came up empty after ten days, so they had to call the search off, and decided that he was probably dead by exposure or animal attack.

A few days later, I was still recuperating from my ordeal when the doorbell rang. When I opened the front door, I burst into tears as Vic limped into my living room.

I kept saying, "Thank God, you're alive." It was shock and happiness rolled into one, and he gave me a hug.

I asked him what had happened, and he said he did hear me call to him from a little distance behind him, and he was about to answer when he stepped into a large hole. He fell forward, struck his head on a rock, and was out cold. He stayed unconscious in that grave until late morning the following day and just lay down with a concussion and sprained ankle. He made a few feeble calls, but I did not answer, and it took days for his dizzy head to get better. His ankle was twice its normal size, and he had to take the lace off that boot. His poncho covered the den, and he had his food and sleeping bag, so just stayed there sleeping most of the time until his light-headed feeling felt somewhat better. The ankle gave him the real problem, for he had to hop down the slope with a branch for a cane. The helicopter could not see him, and he never heard anyone from the search party, since they never got near enough so he could call to them.

"It took me forever to hobble to the off road trail, and my Jeep was gone. I presumed you took it and remembered you had no key. My cell phone battery was dead, and I had hoped to plug it into the Jeep's outlet to recharge it so I could phone 911. I struggled along the muddy trail and finally met a man in a truck who stopped when I yelled. He took me to the police station, and they told me the Jeep was in their car lot. I was able to drive to the hospital for a checkup, because I did not know if the ankle was sprained or broken. The X-ray showed no breaks, but walking on it did not help it any, even though I tried to hop most of the way out."

He said that, as soon as he could hike again, he was going back to the mountain and climb the west slope of Blanco. He thought now that I was a full-fledged hiker and made it out by myself, I must be confident in my directions.

I yelled, "Confident, my God, by the luck of the dumb, I made it home with cold sweat fear as my companion every inch and every foot of that blasted hike. Climb Blanco's west slope? Not in this lifetime. You need a girlfriend who has no sense of danger. Give her a spare key to your Jeep, a two-way radio, a cell phone, and know she is low on brainpower. Marry her, and make sure she is six foot four, so she can keep up with you. Just give me some slob who thinks a walk in the park is a long hike, and who feels an outing is cooking a steak in the backyard. My nightmares still have me camped in the snow, until I wake up shivering from fright. When I find a warm mattress under my hide, I thank God. Let me know what the west side of Blanco looks like. Better yet, take a picture of it for me in living color."

The Line Camp

Being the last hired hand that year at the JJJ Ranch, the worst, lonely job was handed to me with a handshake and good luck from the ranch manager. They had already let off two older cowboys because of their age. The herds were smaller in the hard times of the thirties. I was lucky to have a roof over my head, and my good horse Blue Jay under me, as I headed out to the line camp in the distant mountains.

My pack mules had enough coffee, beans, rice and bacon to last me through the cold winter months, and my rifle would get me fresh game. One mule carried five chickens, and Howard said there were still a few barrels of grain and dry corn at the camp, so I would have the luxury of fresh eggs for breakfast. The large bags of flour would provide the staple for my biscuits and bread, and I would use animal fat for butter. The sugar would add the sweetness to a little cake some cold evening.

It was early October and already the mountains were white with snow as I gained altitude. My horse was huffing a bit in the thin air. As we reached a bend near the river, I could see the cabin near some large pine trees. The barn stood close to the cabin entrance, so it would prove handy in the storms that blew in this higher elevation.

When I walked the animals into their winter quarters, there were four good stalls, with spring hay stacked to the ceiling at the far end. The straw for the bedding was piled in a loose stack, so I could just pitchfork it to the stall floors for bedding underfoot. A large fenced area in the south corner held chickens in past years, and the last hand kept it clean and orderly. My five chickens were placed in the fresh enclosure. They received some corn, grain, and water before I made the mules comfortable. Sue and Josh were always together, so I put them in the large stall next to Blue Jay.

As I walked into the log building, it struck me with a good impression and contained all my needs, with a cot in the corner and a nice kitchen area with a table and chairs. The cook stove was large, and the wood fire chamber was big enough to heat the whole room. Also, the sink was bigger than most, so you could wash your clothes in it and enjoy a sponge bath at times. When I pumped the water handle, a great flow of water poured out in a big gush, so the well seemed to hold an ample supply for watering the animals and me.

The axe and saw leaned against the wall, and though there was a good neat pile of split logs, the winter would demand five times the amount that greeted me. Because it was already quite cold inside the four walls, my match fired up some paper and small pieces of kindling branches. Once burning, I tossed in some large logs. This was going to be home until spring, so I wanted to look over all the supplies stacked in the cabinets, like salt, soap, and matches.

I rode the trail of hoof prints in the snow, which made

it easy to follow some strays that had passed in the trees. By early April, I could round them up and drive them to our south pasture before heading them to the ranch corral. A large number had drifted above me, and some cougar and bear tracks were spotted in unrelated places. The black bear were probably looking for their winter dens.

A deer crossed my rifle sight and was an easy shot within my range as I pulled the trigger. I dressed it out before breakfast and had fresh venison with my eggs for breakfast. Later, I made up my evening meal with the fresh meat and added my potatoes, carrots and onions that had been packed for the trip. Some hand liked to read and left a small library of stories for a winter night, and I would bless him for the company.

While I was feeding my horse and mules, I heard a voice outside the door.

"Hello the barn."

This startled me in my solitary world, and I reached for my gun hanging on a nail before I stuck my head outside in the wind. A lone rider greeted me, using my name. The white beard fooled me, for I recognized Morgan Grant, one of the elderly cowboys that had been let go after I arrived.

He said he was hungry and tried to get work on some of the other ranches, but they weren't taking on hands and thought he was too old for a good day's work. He had no place to go and thought I could use some help with the woodpile and animals. He only wanted a place to bed and some grub, since he had no idea where to turn at his age.

Already, I was lonely for company and had been talking to Blue Jay and the mules. My deer stew was simmering on the back of the stove, so we both had a big plate with some biscuits.

He had a few games he showed me with a deck of cards, and I did not know them and was glad for the company. We fixed up a big pile of straw and put canvas over it for his pallet, and he curled up on it with his first good meal in five days, which put him right to sleep.

In the morning, I could not lift my head off the bunk. My cough shook my body, and my fever left me soaking wet. Morgan made some broth and baked a few biscuits to dip in it, so he sat me up and washed the moisture from my skin and changed my shirt. He was very capable, because he washed my sweat-filled shirt in the sink and hung it near the stove to dry.

He fed the animals and brought in fresh eggs before he cut some of the dead trees and split them for the woodpile. He baked better bread and biscuits than most and kept me alive with his food and care. He would look after me and then scout for fresh game. His rabbit stew was tasty, though I could hardly eat.

Whatever ailment my body picked up hammered my whole system, and in my twenty-six years I never had anything to match it. At times I had trouble breathing and dreams in delirium, so I did not know where I was. Always a cold cloth on my forehead was backed with kind words in some far corner of my mind, and a gentle hand made me sip fresh water from the well.

Now we were into November snowstorms with very cold nights. The stove was full of red flames, and I could hear a thud as a log would drop into the pile of sparks. Morgan kept the room warm for me. In the cold mornings I could hear the rhythm of his axe and the vibration of the saw, as it ran in the back roads of my feverish dreams.

This went on until December, and the meals were always fed to me with the same gentle hands, and some nights the bible was read to me. Since my fever had let up, I was more coherent and could visit with Morgan. He told me about his days as a young cowboy in Arizona, and it sounded so warm and interesting that I longed to go there someday.

My legs would not hold my weight, so he made me crutches at first so I could shuffle my feet in front of me, and later two canes to guide my feeble legs in a dragging walk. I remembered hearing about President Roosevelt's plight with polio and decided that perhaps that is what laid me so low for so long. Morgan rubbed my legs with fat and worked the muscles to keep them moving, since he seemed to know what was needed.

One warm day he got me in the sun, placed me in the saddle aboard Blue Jay, and walked us around the pine trees. It felt so good to be in the fresh air that I at last looked forward to the spring and summer He hobbled the mules in the short grass that stuck up through the melting snow, and they could not stray far from his reach.

Now that spring was approaching with the change in weather, the snow melted slowly and ran down from the higher slopes above the cabin. Morgan thought it was time to ride out of the mountains and get to the ranch. A couple of the hands could come up for the strays in a few weeks, so he told me not to worry about them.

As we dropped into the valley below the cabin, I took my last look at it, knowing I would never return. The lower altitude made for a warmer sun, and by late afternoon we made the ranch gate. The pack mules were behind me, and Morgan took up the rear, but when I turned Blue Jay to face him, his horse had vanished. I scanned the horizon looking for his shape, but could not make out any trace of a silhouette of a horse and rider.

Two of the boys came over to me and took the mules to the barn. My friend Howard realized I was sick and weak and helped me off the horse. When I sat at the bunkhouse table over coffee, I told the hands how lucky I was that Morgan showed up to save my life in my illness. I mentioned all the food he cooked, and the wood he cut, and his gentle hands that washed my wet body. There was a hush around the table, and I guess the boys thought I was still sick, since I lost maybe forty pounds and could hardly walk.

Howard took my hand and slowly walked me to a large cottonwood behind the barn. He told me how Morgan came to the bunkhouse for a meal and a place to bed, and the boys told him to use my bunk. He took me under the tree to a pile of rocks, and a sign on wood.

MORGAN GRANT
BIRTH UNKNOWN
DIED OCT. 1934

He only stayed with the hands a week before he died, and the only thing he left was his bible under your pillow. I asked if it had a slash across the cover that cut the B in half. He could not remember, and when I lifted it to my eyes I recognized the unmistakable mark that I viewed those many cold nights at the line camp.

The Green Pines

This old house was home for my wife and me for forty years. When you have good company like Beth, how could you not be happy? Now that she was in heaven, I found myself in hell. Alone, I was making the coffee, frying bacon and eggs, popping toast, then eating before the television. Then I could hear another voice, but it was definitely a one-way conversation.

Now my kids came by on occasion, and put pressure on me to sell the house and try the new retirement place in town. Did I resist? Of course, but on my own, I went there to the prospective renters' lunch and met my old school chum, Charles David Hicks.

When the receptionist introduced me to the table to my left, I recognized Charlie's name, certainly not the old face. He asked if I was the Ben Hines that went to Johnson High, and we fell into a long conversation about old friends and old times. They had a free seat at his table, so I was off to a comfortable start. There were six seats at the rectangular table, and I was number five.

Charlie asked the gal that gave the renters' tour if he could show me around the place. She thought I would enjoy it better with him, so we went to his digs, and I found it quite nice, with a bedroom, bath, sitting room, television, and very small kitchen.

When I asked if he got tired of cooking and eating breakfast in the morning, he informed me that their buffet spread with eggs, bacon, toast, coffee, and cereal came with the package deal. They ate mostly two meals a day in the dining room in the winter, and on the lovely porch in the summer. Also they had transportation that took in the zoo, Broadway shows, and casinos. When I saw the Olympic pool, tennis courts, and exercise room, I signed right up and put the house on the market.

This was grand living, for they even had a deal with the local golf course to save us money. It took me a while to figure out why all the ladies were so neat. Well, at home in the morning most would probably have no makeup, show curlers in their locks, and brew some coffee in an old housecoat with egg on the collar. It was quite different here, men shaved and dressed up a bit, and we had a civilized outer appearance.

Millie, sort of a blond with white roots, was a flirt to a large degree. Since I was the new kid on the block, she put a little effort into her sparkle. I rather liked the attention and looked forward to the meals just to hear her laugh and give me her pitch.

Charlie clued me in on everyone's background, from so and so the retired funeral director to the president of a large bank. We were all from different worlds on the same playing field. Frankly, I loved being a part of this large retired club, for that brought us all together on common ground, and we shared that same thread of old age.

Millie and I started going out to the events that the home provided, like some new movies, the planetarium, art museums, and outside restaurants. We only received breakfast and dinner each day in our monthly food deal, thus lunch was always left open, unless you wanted to pay extra for it in the dining room. A lot of folks just had a snack in their own kitchen and then an afternoon nap.

Our friendship seemed to get deeper, and we even went to Sunday church together. Of course, I played golf on Wednesdays with Charlie and the boys, so my life was full and happy. The Green Pines was home now, and I loved it.

It was not cheap living on my retirement, and the house still had not sold. I was counting on investing that money to raise my income, so I could coast along in peace. Millie had mentioned marriage a few times, and I skirted that conversation pronto. Some of her stocks were not doing well, so she proposed moving to my furnished house for a while, just to save us both money.

One week back home, and I missed the golf, the pool, the company of men, but mostly the food. Millie thought food came in frozen cartons. The breakfast coffee was burning my gut, and the fried eggs had hard centers.

I knew we had hit a new low when Millie came down one morning in curlers, no makeup, and the housecoat of witches. Purple flowers spread across it like they were growing. I had to excuse myself and drive to McDonald's for a decent cup of coffee and a McMuffin. The coffee was so good, I sat and had a second, and half of a third cup.

When I saw Charlie, he missed my company and complained about his income trying to keep up with expenses.

He mentioned that some of the new two-bedroom apartments were still available, with two baths. They were built for two sisters, or a brother and sister, and maybe a family member. We made a deal for one, since they would take Charlie's one-bedroom unit and put it on the list for people waiting for the smaller apartment.

This worked out fine, and we only shared the kitchen infrequently. Our expenses dropped, as we split the rent and bought food for lunch on occasion. I was back to golf, the pool, and good cooking again. Millie nabbed a boyfriend at the bridge club who had a little money. He bought my house after they were married, since she was still living there. She was happy, and I was overjoyed.

A new, good-looking woman rented Millie's apartment, and now ate at our table. She started making eyes at me and flirting, and I told her I was sorry, but this is where I came in.

Greed

Every morning, ten to twelve of us would meet in Greg's Diner, and we would have coffee together and maybe some toast and eggs. We came for the company and conversation, which was compatible for our retired group. There were three married couples, plus a few of us widows and widowers. It gave us a reason to brush our hair and get a little dressed up and neat in the mornings.

Howard and I sat near one another so we could talk about our hobby, photography, without boring the others. I told him I finally sent for the new digital camera with the four hundred millimeter zoom lens. As soon as it was delivered, I would bring it to the diner to show him. Being on a widow's fixed income from half of my husband's retirement, I could not afford too many luxuries, so had to save nine months to cover the cost of this unnecessary item. I usually only ordered a coffee and Danish most times to stay on my budget, while I listened to George read some of the headlines out loud to us.

When I met the delivery truck in the driveway, he yelled that my package was under the bench behind the plant to hide it. Sure enough, I grabbed it in my hands and opened it before I even got my coat off, for this was one big treat for me.

By morning, I had the camera strap over my neck and my duffle bag with the tripod, extra memory chip, and batteries tucked in the bottom, so I was fully equipped. I had parked behind the Quick Pick roadside store that sold milk, drinks, and some candy and had a couple of gas pumps for this rural area.

When I got into the thick trees, I saw some colorful birds in the zoom lens, and I could fill the screen with a close-up of just the head, the lens was that good. I would snap away, then review the photos on the glass, and then search for the large woodpecker I just spotted a few minutes ago. It was like looking through a pair of binoculars, but the images were sharper.

I ducked behind a large deadfall as a man approached carrying a fair-sized suitcase. He seemed to be checking his back trail and being quite cautious, as he got under a very full tree and slid the case out of sight on a branch in the dense leaves. He retrieved a box and then he quickly hurried back across the brook, and disappeared in the maze of trees.

I heard a car motor accelerate. I moved quickly to the tree and reached up to see what the case contained. When the lid flew open, it took my breath away, for a block of green greeted me with one hundred and fifty dollar bills, all contained in packs held together with elastic bands. I quickly covered my hands with my yellow gloves and took handfuls of the bills and pushed them into my camera bag. I could hardly get most of it inside and was forced to remove the tripod for more space. The weight of my bag bent my back, as I moved along the bank of the brook, with the tripod stuck in between the straps on the bag. My camera was flapping against my chest, as my feet glided in a half run. I did not want to come out where the man entered the woods, so I quickly moved almost across from the store and my parked car.

My right arm ached from the weight of all that heavy paper, and I pushed it into the car trunk and threw my old blanket over it. Now I was afraid to go in the direction my ears told me the car headed, so I drove up the little road behind the store. It was just a dirt lane, and I headed opposite to the location where the man entered the woods. In about an hour, a big Lincoln pulled up, and I had my lens on the driver's seat as I hid in the deep foliage above the road, since the hill was thirty feet higher than the pavement.

A man got out of the passenger side of the car and followed the same direction as the drop-off, and quickly got lost in the trees. He looked like a bulldog, a hit man, and was one scary looking thug. When he came out of the trees, he put both hands up in a gesture that said, "It's not there." The Lincoln did a quick U turn and fled out of sight.

My heart was pumping blood like I ran the distance in the marathon, and realized I was scared to death. Of course, it occurred to me that the money was illegal and some sort of a drug payoff. I felt like running home, but did not want to attract attention in any way, so waited anther hour before I headed out on a different route from the usual one.

When I pulled into my garage, I quickly locked the door and rushed up to my bedroom with the bag and closed my curtains. It was so heavy that I could hardly lift it on my bed. It contained thousands of dollars in neat little stacks, and I did not touch it until I again wore my gloves, for I did not want sweaty prints on any part of these unlawful greenbacks.

Where to put it, entered my thoughts, as a closet could

be robbed, and then someone could put the finger on me. I waited until morning so the attic would have some natural light from the window. It would not be wise to have a flashlight showing its beam through the glass. Yes, I was saturated with caution and paranoia.

Early in the morning, after hardly any sleep I opened a large box of envelopes near my desk and started making up packages with twenty thousand dollars in each one. They were in neat thousand dollar packs, so they were easy to separate. It was a little awkward with the gloves and took me hours to complete the task. I used a sponge to seal the glue, so my saliva would not spread my DNA across the envelopes.

My attic had a few boards down the middle of the large space, so you could walk from either end and not touch the open two-by-fours, with just the plaster showing from the bedroom ceilings below. I was careful not to stray off the ramp, as I took the full envelopes from the pile and carefully slid them under the walkway boards. It took me most of the morning to get them out of sight, because my knees had arthritis, and I had to crawl around on the plywood to complete the operation.

It occurred to me that I could never suddenly start buying new cars or furniture without drawing attention to this poor widow. I had changed the peaceful quality of my life and exchanged it with fear. Why didn't I just leave the suitcase where the man left it and mind my own business? My body was now so wet from fright and work that I headed for the shower. I wondered if my friends at Greg's missed me at the long table.

When the phone rang, I could hardly control my hello on a natural level, as I mustered a greeting. It was just a neighbor telling me about the sale of ten cans of soup for a dollar.

Now the money could rot in the attic and maybe never be found, even after I passed on to Heaven, and maybe Hell now. If found after my death, I would be labeled a drug dealer, and what would my daughter and son think of me?

Calm down lady, use your brain, and think. Yes, I could be like Robin Hood, for I could give to the poor and steal from the druggies. Sure, laugh, but I knew a safe and happy ending to the whole mess. The more I thought about it, the smarter it seemed, and it ate at my sense of morality. I retrieved the envelopes by lying nose down on the plywood walkway.

I took my address list to the library computer with the printer and brought my own paper, so I could type out the name and each address for a local charity. There was the Salvation Army, the soup kitchen, churches, boys' club, homeless shelter, and on and on, until I had more than the money envelopes could cover. After I cut the addresses and names off the list, I glued them on the face of the envelopes and resealed them with scotch tape to make sure they were secure across the back seams, and had to use thin rubber gloves to perform the task. However, I did relent and buy the postage stamps with the drug money after I weighed the little stacks on the desk postage scale.

In the evening, I had them in a cardboard box on the passenger seat of my car.

I never drove with such caution. Leaving home, I moved on the highway and put distance between my front door, as I moved in the direction of Huntersville, a larger town with a main post office and a few mailboxes, where I could just drive up and drop my load. Then I could move away in the cover of darkness. My gloved hands were shaking as I wiped the sweat from my forehead with the back of the pigskin.

A few days later, everyone was friendly at the diner for the morning coffee, and George always had his newspaper news to report to the gang with local stories. When he mentioned a Mafia figure was found dead with a bullet between his eyes, the police thought it was a drug deal that went sour. When he put the paper down, I could see the man's photo on the front page, and even upside down I recognized the mustache and image as the deliveryman in the woods.

It hit me hard that his death was surely due to my stupidity, drug dealer or not, and I would have to live with it. Lord, yes, a dumb broad named Grace stole for the first time in her life and became a gun moll in her greed, though she didn't actually pull the trigger. Sally asked me why I was perspiring in the cool restaurant, and I laughed and said it was just the remnants of a hot flash.

She said, "Amen to that," and the gang chuckled.

In a few days, things were back to normal, and George said, "Listen to this," and started reading about the donations that rolled into most of the coffers of the town's charities, and started listing them. "No one knows the identity of the philanthropist, but they wish to thank him, or her, in the paper and express their appreciation for the fine support in this depressed economy."

My second hot flash was creeping up on me, and I instantly stood and announced I had to get some food for lunch at the grocery store. I popped fifty cents in the newspaper machine in front of the restaurant and read the whole story while I was parked in front of the supermarket.

Because there were a few robberies in the neighborhood, I started worrying about the two gold coins I had in an old sock in my desk. Now that I had a good safe place to hide things, I got on my hands and knees on the platform in the attic and started to push it under the plywood a distance of a foot. My hands hit something that blocked my entrance, and when I put my nose down to the space with the flashlight, I spotted three packs of hundreds I had missed.

When I pulled them out of the envelopes, I realized my gloves were in the kitchen. It was too late now, and I could no longer even think of sending money out to any organization, since my sweaty hands had tainted the money when they came into contact with the paper. Besides, the FBI, IRS, or local police could be checking the mail drops looking for the mystery person involved with so much cash. My DNA had dropped its scent on the bills, or was I just a middle-aged, stupid woman with too many forensic television shows under my belt.

I stayed in the house all day with the doors locked. It was a cool fall night, so I lit a fire and sat holding the sixty thousand dollars in my sweaty palms thinking about my car payments, Blue Cross, electric, gas and water bills, as I kept looking at all the money with the large numbers printed on their faces. The nervous fear of the last week hit me all at once, as tears poured down my cheeks, nose, and splashed on the front of my blouse while I counted to ten. Then with one sweep of my hand I threw the money on top of the burning logs. As the paper curled and twisted in the flames, there was no turning back, and I thought, "You won't need a sleeping pill tonight, Gracie."

The Maxwell Brand

Mr. Randolph Maxwell made his fortune in shipping out of San Francisco to the Orient. Every man has his dream, and when he retired, he searched for a small western ranch so he could have some horses and cattle, wear his new boots and big hat, and become a gentleman rancher as he rode a nice gentle horse. We were surrounded by ranches of one hundred and thirty thousand acres to almost two hundred thousand, and some with one hundred and fifty horses in the remuda. The Maxwell brand had more of a string of horses we were so small, and only maybe sixty cows to start a herd.

Most of the big operations had cowboys with wives and families and housing for them surrounding the headquarters. We had a small bunkhouse that bedded five young men from sixteen to twenty one. The Hurd twins were both eighteen. Mr. Stan McGuire (Mac) was sixty, an old time cowboy with ranching knowledge, and he really ran the operation, since Mr. Maxwell only could play at it from western books. Mac bunked with us and made saddles for his enjoyment, and they were truly better than any from the best western store in Montana.

Mrs. Hill, or Annie to us, and her lovely niece Clara

cooked our meals in the cookhouse only twenty feet from our sleeping quarters. We built a long hallway from our side door to the kitchen and sitting room so we could stay out of the blizzard winds and snows to get to our meals. Their sleeping quarters were attached to the back of the cookhouse west wall. The kitchen was open with just a half wall and shelf separating it from our long eating table. The women put the food in deep dishes on the counter for meals, mashed potatoes, beef, vegetables, bread, and always some canned fruit. A cake or pie might sit at the end of the counter with a pile of cookies, and we helped ourselves to the buffet.

We were all at an age to appreciate Clara's looks and sweet disposition, and maybe most of us had a crush on her. The only sparks that reached out to any of us went to Rowdy, so named because he was the quiet one, and the opposite of his nickname. He and Clara exchanged love notes and recipes, since his mother had polio and was in a wheelchair; thus he did a lot of cooking for her when his sisters were too young to pitch in. This gave him an edge on us, for they first got talking via some dinner recipe Annie whipped up one Sunday dinner.

The fly in the ointment, or burr under our saddles, was Randolph Junior, since he was the spoiled son given the job to ride herd over us. He would come in for coffee just to see Clara and bring her some fudge his mother made, or the Chinese cook, Gong, produced. We would usually stop our table talk and sip our coffee in silence as he made his play for Clara, and he was self conscious of our concentration on his presence. Of course, that was our way of irritating him for anything too obvious could get us fired, and this was in the hard times of the early forties and we needed our jobs. We all were raised on some of the neighboring ranches, so this life was nothing new to us since most of us help ride herd at eight years old and had been raised in a saddle so to speak.

When Randolph first came in, Clara was still talking to Rowdy at the other end of the counter, and she was reading one of his notes and then slipped it into the large homemade pocket on her apron. When she walked over to Randolph she offered him some dessert with his coffee, and he presented her with something special from the main house, but slipped his hand in the pocket and retrieved the note and did a sleight of hand to shove it in his pocket. I spotted it right off, but Rowdy put his finger to his lips and smiled.

When we left Annie and Mac drinking a cup of coffee, he was doing a fancy stitch on the saddle pommel. He always stayed up later than the rest of us to work with his leather and visit with Annie who fussed over him.

When we were into our morning coffee waiting for chow, Rowdy told Mac he saw Randolph lift his note from Clara's pocket. When Rowdy told him it was his Mother's recipe for blueberry tarts, Mac exploded into laughter and we of course joined in. When Randolph slipped in for a coffee excuse to see Clara, Mac asked him if he made his mother a blueberry tart. We just about died laughing as his face turned red, and he pushed his cup away from him so fast it spilled. Then he hurried out the door. He could fire us, but not Mac, for the operation would fold up in a week without his know how.

Randolph had talked Clara into going to the Saturday night dance in town, and she only considered it because she wanted to see some of her old friends there, and she was young. Rowdy swallowed the pain of that information, but he could not take her since none of us had cars. At ten below zero, no one would consider riding to town ten miles away in those temperatures, and certainly Clara could never make the trip. Randolph had his father's cars and trucks at his disposal, so that was a bitter pill for Rowdy.

The following week Mac asked Mr. Maxwell for the car so he could take Annie into town, and of course he invited Rowdy and Clara to join them. The young ones went to the dance while Annie and Mac visited friends. Randolph and his father had a fight over this, and Gong gave us all the details of the yelling back and forth between father and son. Randolph made the mistake of telling Mac off for interfering with his relationship with Clara and came on a little bit too strong.

Mac grabbed him by his shirt, almost lifted him off the ground, and slapped him as hard as you can without calling it a punch. Randolph had tears in his eyes and went home. The Hurd twins saw this incident, and we enjoyed the story from each of their lips for most of the night. Rowdy was thrilled to hear the details, and it was the best night of camaraderie among our group in a long time.

Saturday morning Mac pulled it off again with the car so he could take the girls shopping early when the shops opened, and he needed Rowdy to carry the heavy flour and sugar bags. Mac had Rowdy lined up for a job at a friend's ranch near Billings, and he slipped him a hundred dollars so he could marry Clara. After the ceremony, Mac put them on the twelve o'clock train heading southwest from our town of Forsyth. Then Mac decided to marry Annie, so they went back to see his friend Judge Miller, and he tied the knot for them. The judge asked him why they did not make it a double ceremony, and Mac said,

"I only got the idea when I stood up for Rowdy."

When he came back to the ranch, Randolph came into the kitchen to see Clara to give her a ring, but Mac had the pleasure of telling him that she married Rowdy, and they both left on the noon train for his job on a ranch in Billings. Randolph called him an SOB and quickly ran up to the main house. The cowhands celebrated the marriage of both of them with a big handshake and joy at seeing the boss run home to complain that Clara married that no good cowboy, Rowdy.

The next day was Sunday and very cold with some blowing snow. We all sat in the sitting room in the kitchen listening to the radio, as Mac and Annie sat together, and we watched him work on the saddle with a radio story in the background. When they interrupted the program, they said Pearl Harbor was under attack by Japanese planes. To be honest, we had to ask Mac where Pearl Harbor was, and what did it mean. Mac's nephew was stationed in the Navy there, and he said, "Sorry boys, we are at war. Hawaii is an American possession."

After December seventh, one by one we faded from the ranch, for the Navy, Coast Guard, Marines, and Army took us all. Rowdy ended up in the Pacific Islands in the infantry and was wounded enough to return to Clara alive. The only men left on the ranch were Mac, Gong, Mr. Maxwell, and Randolph who was trying to get an exemption. Too bad for Randolph, for the Army took him away to an infantry basic training camp on the West Coast. After basic, he received his first leave, but did not come home to see his parents. In fact, he went AWOL never to be seen again, and we suspected he drifted over the border into Mexico. Mr. Maxwell sold off the cattle and horses, except for his heavy wagon team and his favorite Tennessee Walker with the nice gait.

Mrs. Maxwell died a short time later and was heartbroken about Randolph's disappearance. Mr. Maxwell was so ashamed of his son's cowardice actions that he never mentioned his name again. Annie sent us all cookies, and Mac wrote to every one of us and kept us currant on news of one another. The Hurd twins were both killed in action. One died from a bullet in the Pacific Theater, and the other caught a large piece of shrapnel in the invasion on Omaha Beach.

Annie was in her forties when she married Mac, but she produced him a son named Stanton McGuire the third. We received many photos of him through the war years, so his photo made Europe, New Guinea, to the Pacific Islands. We all have that connection to the ranch to this day and still write one another, though we live with our families in different parts of the west. Mac is having a reunion this summer, so we will all get together with our children and wives. We will miss the Hurd twins, and I am afraid Randolph won't be there, since he is probably sitting in some little Mexican village waiting for his father to die. Then he will resurface to claim his ranch and money. Too bad sonny, but daddy already legally turned it over to Mac and Annie, and thinks Stan Junior is the grandson he never had, and plays with him every day.

Life goes on for all of us, but those were the innocent days of our youth, and we recall them through our photos, letters, and souvenirs of remembrance.

Margaret

She was a lovely lady of the old school, maybe seventy-nine or eighty, but she never did reveal her age to me. Since she was a widow with no children, I was her only friend at this time in life. She could manage her small physical needs and do her skimpy meals, like one egg for her morning energy, and on a good day perhaps one piece of toast with it. Soup usually carried her through to her evening snack of crackers and cheese, so you can see she was not a big, robust woman. Still she could walk behind a grocery cart for balance and would wander around the store picking up her few items for her weekly subsistence. I usually followed her at a distance to make sure she could manage her measly choice of a tin of tuna here, a can of tomato soup, and maybe two bananas.

She lived behind me across the back alley in a two-car garage that was converted into a little house during the war, and the location allowed the town fathers to let it pass code as a dwelling. It was very handy for Margaret, for she could take care of the small sitting room next to the kitchen, with just two chairs and an old sofa, plus dust her few tables and wash a cup and dish for her few real meals. The only other room in the place housed her bed and a tiny bathroom. God knows what rent that small area would bring to the owner.

Her husband was killed in the war, and they never had enough time to produce a family because he was in the army on leave when they were married. Off he went with his regiment one week after the marriage certificate was framed, and she never saw him again.

I suspected that her income consisted of a very small social security check, because her only job for all those years was behind a counter in a five and ten cent store, until the poor sales closed the place as the larger department stores drifted into the area. Everything that could be purchased in the dime store could be bought in a number of the new outlets that opened in the shopping centers on the edge of town, and they were maybe a few cents cheaper.

She did not have a phone, so I would take over some of my cookies and cake at times and tell her I was going shopping. Margaret jumped at the chance for a ride, because the grocery store was several miles from her location. When we would have tea at her small table off the kitchen cube, I would get her to talk about her childhood on a Canadian farm. Her father had milk cows, and since their farm was the first one from the village, they could walk to school and the library. Because I always wanted to live on a farm with the animals, I would drag the childhood stories from her old memory. Her brothers each had a toboggan, and the three of them would help their father milk in the morning before school. They had a route in town with their own customers, and the boys pulled the large milk containers to the individual homes in the snow. The families had their own bottles, and the brothers would ladle out one or two quarts to fill their needs with fresh milk for that day. They received ten cents for each Canadian quart. During the warm months, they had little wagons for their trips with the milk supply.

Her father had two large mixed blood heavy horses. They would pull the hay wagon at times. The boys forked manure from it to fertilize the fields and would work those heavy pitchfork loads until their muscles ached. She would bring them lemonade on the hot days, and they were always happy to see her wave with the pitcher in her hand as they wiped the sweat from their dirty foreheads. She and her mother had a big tub that was filled once a week with the flour and bread mixture that would last for seven days. Margaret's job was to mix it thoroughly so her mother could drop it in the bread pans to rise and bake enough loaves for three hungry boys, a husband, Margaret and herself. Also, they made cakes, muffins, and cookies and saved some for Sundays as the minister just might drop in for tea for a visit with the family in the clean parlor.

In my thoughts, I would drift into the farmhouse with her and visualize life in the small village in this large brick house surrounded by a sturdy porch, swing and all. They had the chickens for fresh eggs, butter from the cows, pigs for a ham once in a while, and a few sheep, but mostly the milk business put money in the cookie jar in the kitchen. Clothes and shoes were cheap in those days, so the ten cents a quart would add up to a nice sum with the amount of milk their cows produced twice a day.

It always did amaze me that she suddenly had an appetite, when I brought my few baked items for our tea, and I did wonder if she could not afford more food in her cart, or that my company induced the craving for cake and cookies.

I have always loved large workhorses, since I saw a

heavy horse show at a Canadian fall fair when we were visiting my husband's family in Ontario. Margaret said when she was young the only way she could climb up on old Pat's back was to have a high box to use for a step. Once she fell off his back in town and had to walk him around the village until she found something she could stand on to regain her riding position. He was so broad her legs stuck out East and West as she rode the dirt trail home.

We were all upset at two murders that took place a week apart not far from our location. Both victims were elderly women, and he killed them with a rope around the neck. When a third eighty-five-year-old woman was put to death in her bed, the police thought they had a serial killer prowling our quiet streets. I asked Margaret if she wanted to sleep in my house, but she had no fear at all. When I came over for our snack, she was using her pitchfork to turn the soil, and she would sit down on a small stool for a few minutes and bury some tomato plants in the black earth. She smiled and said, "Once a farmer, always a farmer."

Finally I bought her a cheap cell phone with paid minutes so she could at least phone me for help if she fell or needed aid. She was so appreciative of anything I did for her, that it made me feel good in my heart. With so little in life, she had a happy attitude that shone through her voice and glowing face. I let her know if any stranger bothered her, she could phone 911 or phone me, and I made her memorize my phone number. After repeating it a few times, her old brain was better at numbers than my sixty-odd-years gray matter, so I felt content to let her stay in her own familiar surroundings. She pulled out a baseball bat and said she would sleep with it, and put her pitchfork under her bed and laughed.

That conversation came back to haunt me a few weeks later when she phoned me at eight in the morning on a Sunday. It seems she heard a noise in the kitchen with a big bang right after it. Her door was kicked in, and the rude homeless man that begged for bills outside the stores in town flicked the bedroom light on and said, "I want your money, now." He grabbed her hands behind her back and tied them together with a nylon stocking.

She said, "What do you want with a ninety-eight-year-old women that has no cash at all?"

I said, "You are not ninety-eight."

She replied, "You know that, and I know that, but I thought if I acted real old, he would not hurt me. He started looking in my bureau drawers, and while he was scavenging through my underwear, I reached back to the table, got the scissors in my right hand and snipped the nylon slowly until I had freed both hands. The baseball bat was under my blanket, and I sat there like an old helpless woman as he started picking out my private keepsakes from the little chest on the floor. When I saw my husband's gold watch come up in his view, as he studied it, bang, I knocked him cold flat on the floor with a homerun swing of the bat and dialed 911 to the police. He sort of came to and stared at me, but I had the pitchfork in my hands by then and told him, 'Leave my husband's watch on the floor, for he asked me to keep it for him when he went off to war.' By then the police walked in the open front door and put cuffs on him. They read him his rights and warned him that they would check his DNA on the murdered women and hold him for attacking this nice lady. He answered, 'She's not so nice, look at my head.'"

All the shops, banks, gas stations and such had chipped in for a reward of five thousand dollars, and some of the department stores had gift certificates added to the money. Margaret's smiling face was in the local paper as the mayor presented the reward check to her with the merchants in the background. After she took it to her bank for cash, she asked me if I could take her to the grocery store. When I followed her through the rows of food, I was shocked to see a large roast, lamb chops, bags of flour, sugar, two boxes of butter, eggs, bread, potatoes, fresh vegetables, and jams. By the time we unloaded the pile into my car, I had to back up to her back door, so we could carry them all into the kitchen. She said I must stay for lunch, started the meal instantly, pulled out two steaks from the meat pile, and dropped a blueberry pie on the table.

I thought I was a good eater, but it was like Thanksgiving and Christmas put together for her sudden appetite, and did she enjoy that meal smiling at me through every bite, yes indeed. She informed me that she would save most of the money to add a few extra dollars each week to her food bill, and she intended to savor her meals until it ran out.

The local little league baseball team gave her a gold baseball bat one of the fathers painted, and presented it to her with a red ribbon on the handle. She was the town hero for weeks, and I was truly proud to be her neighbor.

I told her how surprised I was that she had the courage to use the baseball bat on the intruder. She informed me that she was ready to give him a stab with her scissors and the pitchfork next if he started to get to his feet. She bragged, "After all, I am a tough raised farm girl that used to roughhouse with my three brothers, and I kept them in line until they were in high school.

Gosh, I have to send my last living brother a picture of his sis on the front page of the newspaper. He'll show it to all his friends in the retirement home. As soon as my tomatoes are ripe, we'll have lunch with a garden salad." She chuckled, "I suddenly don't feel ninety anymore, and that is my true age."

LaVergne, TN USA
09 November 2009
163453LV00003B/5/P